A SIMPLE COUNTRY DECEPTION

BLYTHE BAKER

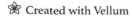 Created with Vellum

~

The violent death of a friend plunges Helen Lightholder into another case of danger and deceit as she struggles to unravel the truth behind the grisly killing. With her own past continuing to haunt her, Helen works to uncover the ultimate answer behind the mystery that has plagued her since the beginning.

Return to the quaint - and deadly - village of Brookminster a final time for the dramatic conclusion to Helen's adventures.

~

1

The first of September swept through England like a whisper. Hardly noticed by anyone, apart from the school children, the trees began to change from their vibrant greens to the rich coppers, scarlets, and golds. The rains had slowed, but the dull, steely grey clouds decided to stay, blanketing Brookminster in a quiet stillness.

Life around Brookminster had been rather enjoyable, as of late. With Sidney being gone, and the murder of Mr. James behind us, I was a little surprised, and yet at the same time relieved, that life had gone back to a sense of normalcy.

The haberdashery was booming, as people began to prepare for the holidays that were around the corner. Mothers wished to send important bits and bobs to their sons off serving in the war, or wanted to customize the sweaters they had spent months knitting for them for Christmas in order to remind them of home. Wives began to pull their family's winter clothing from the attic, and after dusting them off, realized they needed patching, or new buttons, or ribbons without stains.

I had more orders than I knew what to do with, but I was pleased with my work. It was a much more pleasant way to spend my days than looking for murderers and running for my life.

"Thank you, Mrs. Georgianna," I said with a wave as the kindly woman made her way to the front door of the shop.

She returned the gesture with a smile, and the bell above the door chimed as she stepped out into the cool, cloudy afternoon.

I pushed the box of navy buttons back onto the shelf beside its brethren, straightening it so it sat flat.

The clock on the wall began to sing its hourly song, and with a sigh of relief, I realized it was three o'clock. Time to close up for the day.

Life was certainly beginning to feel normal, at least in the small village. The world at large was still at war, and I did my best to keep myself abreast of what was happening, but most of it was so troubling that it did nothing except make my stomach churn.

The only positive side of having such troubling times in our own town had been that everyone's focus was forced inward. In its absence, it was much easier to see the evidence around us that the war was waging. People had family members serving, some of whom had not been heard from in weeks. Smiles were still exchanged, but I noticed how strained most of them seemed.

The same thoughts passed through everyone's mind; when would it end? And what would it ultimately cost?

Nevertheless, everyone attempted to carry on with

their daily lives. After all, laundry still needed doing, and meals still needed cooking. Shops still served the towns-folk the goods they needed, and the children continued their education in the small schoolhouse down near the river.

I collected my ration coupons from the drawer in my kitchen, checking my pantry for the goods I absolutely needed. Since the war began, I found myself drifting to my grandmother's cookbook, filled with recipes of few ingredients that were satiating and easy. I'd become quite efficient at making the most of the limited amount of food I was allotted during the week, and had even begun making extras for others in town, like the Driscoll's and the Diggory's.

I scrawled a few items down onto a piece of paper, including some flour, salt, molasses, and gelatin, and tucked it into the pocket of my jacket. I shrugged it on and headed out into the dreary afternoon.

It didn't take me long to make it to the grocer's, and just like every other Monday afternoon, I saw the same customers looking for the same items. Monday meant that canned vegetables were buy one, get one can free. While I wasn't all that fond of canned green peas, they were much easier to use than the fresh peas that I'd already picked from my back garden, and canned for the winter. I had never considered myself much of a gardener before moving to Brookminster, but Irene had taught me a great deal...as had Sidney Mason, despite the fact that he betrayed me, in the end.

I was beginning to enjoy my life in the village, and for the first time ever, it felt like *my* life. Not the life I lived with my parents, and not even the life I'd started with my husband, Roger. It was a life I'd chosen for myself, and I had built it the way I'd seen fit.

I glanced over my shoulder, out the window of the shop into the street, my eyes scanning the shadows of the alleyway between the two shops on the opposite side of the road like they always did.

Are you there, Roger? Are you still watching me?

It had been weeks since I'd seen him. The flower he left in the low cobblestone wall between the buildings in town was safely pressed between the pages of a book that I kept on my bedside table. There had been no clues, no notes, not indication that he was still in town.

I wasn't surprised, of course. Even though I didn't know the specifics of his secret mission, or what it was exactly that kept us apart, I knew that he had made the effort to reach out to me and let me know he was still alive, likely going against orders to do so.

Even still, I wanted to see him. I found myself waking in the middle of the night at the slightest sound, wondering if he had finally come home to me. The more I thought of it, the more I realized I wanted it.

I had believed the war had taken him from me forever. Knowing now that wasn't true, I wanted nothing more than to reconcile with him, and to find some way to pick up where we left off together.

There was nothing in that alleyway outside, just like there hadn't been for weeks now. I supposed I just needed to be all right with that, and accept it for what it was...for now.

If I was honest with myself, I would have seen that I was, in fact, afraid of something happening to Roger. A German spy had so easily infiltrated my life, and the little village of Brookminster, that it made me realize anyone could be a spy undercover, and I would never know. What if one of these spies caught up to Roger? Noticed him watching me? Communicating with me? What would they do? Was Roger putting himself at risk by revealing himself to me? If he watched me as closely as I believed he did, then how could I be sure someone else wasn't watching him as closely?

These were the same questions that chased themselves around inside my mind at all hours of the day. It seemed I could never find reprieve from them.

Not only that, but I found I had nothing but questions in my life ever since Roger's supposed death.

I paid for my groceries and stepped back out into the late afternoon day.

As the sun began to make its way toward the horizon, I discovered I was among many who were out taking care of errands and other responsibilities before the day came to a close. Mrs. Taylor ushered home her sons, both of whom had very long faces, likely having been pulled away from playing with their friends well past their supper time. Mr. Trent was out watering his mums with a bright green watering can, something his wife must have recently repainted. Mr. and Mrs. Henrietta were out for an evening stroll, Mrs. Henrietta carrying a lovely blue parasol, even though there was no sun to block from her fair skin. Mr. Henrietta held tightly to the leash of their Great Dane, Sanford, who was all too happy to tug against his restraints to come and sniff the edges of my jacket.

"Good evening, Mrs. Lightholder," Mrs. Henrietta

said, smiling kindly at me as they slowed to a stop outside the grocer's. "How are you this fine evening?"

"I'm quite well, thank you," I said, bending over to give Sanford the appropriate greeting of scratches behind his floppy, black ears. "And how are you both doing?"

"Just fine, all things considered," Mr. Henrietta said. "Just said goodbye to the Mayfields."

"Goodbye?" I asked, my brow furrowing. "Where are they going?"

"Oh, just a trip to see their son out in Hertfordshire, nothing serious. He works for a company that's been supplying the military with ammunition. Foul work, I tell you, but they haven't seen him in months. This war has been demanding so much of our young people…"

"Yes, it certainly has," I said, frowning.

Sanford licked at the underside of my hand with his wet, sloppy tongue.

"They'll be back by next Monday, though, old Jim's got his own responsibilities down at the meadery," Mr. Henrietta said.

"That, and Karen Smith's wedding is next weekend," Mrs. Henrietta said with a nod. "Mrs. Mayfield would certainly never miss her own niece's ceremony."

"Too true, my dear," Mr. Henrietta said. "Though I can't blame them for wanting to leave town for a bit, eh? Awfully nice that things have been as quiet as they have been as of late."

"Don't say such things," Mrs. Henrietta said with a jab of her elbow to his ribs.

"I agree, though," I said, wiping as much of the slobber off my hands onto Sanford's side as I could while he happily panted and sniffed. "I hope that we can have a quiet few months before Christmas. And who knows? Maybe we will be able to see the end of the war coming sooner rather than later."

"We can only hope, my dear, we can only hope," Mrs. Henrietta said heavily.

Something behind me caught her attention, causing a perplexed expression to pass over her face.

I glanced over my shoulder to follow her gaze, and saw Inspector Sam Graves walking toward us.

"Good evening, Inspector," Mr. Henrietta said with a casual salute up at the man who was easily twice his height and width. "Good to see you out of the station for once."

"I couldn't agree more," Sam said, giving Mr. Henrietta a nod of acknowledgement. He gave me a sidelong smile before inclining his head to Mrs. Henrietta. "And you are looking well this evening, Margaret."

"Oh, thank you, Inspector, as are you," she said. "Well, Helen dear, it was lovely to catch up with you. Do call me soon so we can schedule a time for tea, won't you?"

"Of course," I said. "I look forward to it."

She smiled as she and her husband started off back down the road, tugging Sanford along regretfully behind them.

"A lovely couple," Sam said. "It's too bad their son moved off to America. I know they miss him terribly."

I studied him for a moment. "You really seem to know everyone in this village, don't you?"

He met my gaze with his own piercing blue one, the same steadiness and stoic nature revealed there as always. "Yes, I suppose I do," he said. "Though it certainly is part of my job. It's better to know them and understand them than to be caught off guard when someone does something surprising."

I arched an eyebrow at him.

He shrugged, looking away. "It's true, and you know it is, as much as you don't like to admit that people, even good people, make mistakes sometimes."

I sighed. "Will you ever have a more cheerful view of the world?" I asked.

He gave me a sly grin. "Perhaps one day, when I am far removed from my post, and have spent a great deal of time on my own out in nature, with nothing but the trees and the babbling brooks for company."

I considered arguing with him for a moment about how lonely that life was sure to be, but then realized the romantic idealism of it. "I suppose..." I decided on.

"Where might you be heading this evening?" he asked me, sliding his hands into the pockets of his trousers.

"Home, I suppose," I said, lifting a grocery bag so he could see. "I'd rather not carry these around all night."

"May I walk you home?" he asked.

There was something so juvenile, so innocent about his words that it caught me off guard. He never struck me as the sort of man to ask for permission for things. Instead, he simply just did as he saw he needed to, and would make amends later if needed.

"Yes, all right," I said, smiling at him.

Before I could stop him, he stooped and took the bags from my hands, tucking them into the crook of his arm. "No sense in making a lady carry these heavy bags."

My face turned pink. "Well...thank you," I said, and we set off up the street together.

Our mutual companion was silence for a short time.

Dogs barked and mothers called out to their children. Bike bells chirped, and a car engine thrummed to life a few streets over.

"How's business been lately?" Sam asked finally, his voice breaking the tense quiet between us.

"Quite good, thank you," I said, my hands clasped tightly in front of me, as I was uncertain what else to do with them. "I've recently been able to expand my available items for sale, including new sewing needs and even a few machines, as well as some very fine threads made of spun silk to use. I haven't been able to keep them in stock, and – " the color in my cheeks deepened. "I'm sorry, you probably don't want to hear about all that."

"On the contrary, I find your business fascinating," he said. "Far less troublesome than my line of work."

I smiled. "Well, that much is for certain. I've been pleased to have the chance to focus on my business and not be chasing after some...well, *someone* who has committed some sort of terrible crime."

Sam laughed. "Certain men at the station think quite the opposite. They're becoming rather bored with the lack of excitement around here lately. I heard one threatening to transfer over to London, saying he had vital experience that could help them catch the most dastardly of criminals there."

"They cannot be serious," I said. "Would they rather our village be overrun with criminals, with crime, and death?"

"They are the young ones. The ones who are brave, and have no sense yet," Sam said, shaking his head. "The ones who really haven't experienced the gruesome side of their jobs yet."

"How is it that I have experienced more than they have?" I asked. "I'm not even on the police force."

"I know," Sam said. "But you have seen more than most people should have to in their whole lives. You lost your husband, discovered the truth about your aunt, and attempted to show compassion to someone fleeing the war, only to find greed and selfishness rearing their ugly heads and stealing lives away."

I frowned. "It makes my life sound ideal when you put it that way," I said sarcastically.

"I never said it was," he said. "But you have learned to use your experiences to your advantage, instead of allowing the fear to control you and drive you away."

I let out a low, hollow chuckle. "You don't know me very well then, do you?" I asked. "You aren't there in the middle of the night when the nightmares come, and – " I cut myself off, pulling away from the vulnerability.

"I understand all too well..." he said.

My house appeared ahead, the silence falling between us once again.

"Someone was asking about Sidney's house, you know," Sam said as we came to a stop right outside the gate to my front garden. "A young family with children, hoping to escape the outskirts of London, for reasons I'm sure you can imagine."

A chill ran down my spine as I looked up at the cottage, the memories of the night Sidney died by my hand all too clear and easy to recall. I shook my head. "Do they know what happened there?" I asked. "I'm not certain anyone would buy it if they knew."

"It's not the house's fault," Sam said. "Besides, if everyone knew the full history of the houses they bought,

I doubt anyone would ever step foot inside anything that wasn't brand new. Life happens within the walls, but when those lives move on, new lives can step in and the house continues on, unaffected. Look at you, for instance. You know that your aunt was killed in your home, yet you still continue to live there."

"Yes, but that doesn't mean I don't struggle with it still," I said. "Often, I just do my best to not think about it. But I see your point. How can we be sure that the houses we choose have not been tainted in some way?"

"If anything, his house is a testament to your strength," Sam said. "Your refusal to give up. What happened that night is proof that good does win in the end, and that is a story of hope."

I stared up into his face, the golden light of the setting sun making the blue of his eyes look almost green.

He really was a handsome man, with a good heart and a fierce sense of duty and loyalty. There were few like him in the world.

"Well...thank you for the encouragement, Mr. Graves," I said, smiling at him.

"You're quite welcome," he said, smiling back. He rubbed the back of his neck with his hands, staring up at my cottage, which was the color of honey in the evening light. "Helen, now that things seem to have calmed down around here, I...well, I've been wondering about something."

Something in the change of his tone caught my attention. I looked up at him, my heart skipping a few beats. What was he getting at?

"...Yes?" I asked, my palms beginning to sweat.

"I certainly do not wish to be presumptuous, or to

come on too strong, but...I was wondering if you might be interested in a meal together...sometime?"

I stared up at him, my mouth going dry. He wanted to go out somewhere together?

"Of course, it doesn't need to be anything fancy," he said. "I just thought it might be nice if we were to spend time together outside of a crime scene. I think we get along together quite well."

I licked my lips. I would have been lying if I told myself this was completely unexpected. It certainly wasn't, not after his request to take me to lunch which ended up being nothing more than a means to discuss a case. I'd prepared myself as if it was a romantic occasion, however, and part of me had hoped it would be.

But then Roger reappeared, and all thoughts of any romantic feelings I might have had for Sam were thrown clear out the window. How could I think of another man when the one I'd given my heart to, my promise of my life to, was still alive?

"I think we get along together well, too, Sam," I said. "And I – "

"Helen, there you are!"

Sam and I turned to see Irene Driscoll walking down the street toward me, Michael following along right after her.

"Irene," I said, somewhat grateful, and yet simultaneously annoyed at her timing. "Is everything all right?"

"Well, yes," she said. "I've been looking for you for the past hour. I telephoned your house, no one answered, and then I thought you might be at the grocer's, since you said you needed to go this evening and get a few things. You weren't there, either."

She stopped on the other side of the fence, and when she realized who it was I was standing with, her brow furrowed.

"Oh, please...don't tell me there's been another crime– "

"No, not at all," Sam said, smiling at Irene. He then looked over at me, and set my groceries down at my feet. "Just...think about what I said, all right? Feel free to call me whenever you've made up your mind. You ladies have a good night."

And with that, he deftly stepped out of the gate, and started back up the road toward the center of town.

Irene arched her brow, giving me a pointed look. "What was he doing here?" she asked.

I watched him go, my heart in my throat. "You won't believe this, but he asked me if I wanted to go to dinner with him sometime. I didn't give him an answer."

Irene's face paled. "That was my fault, wasn't it?"

"No, it's all right," I said. "To be honest, I wasn't really sure how to even answer him."

"I thought things were going so well between you two," she said. "It's been clear he has feelings for you for some time now."

"Yes, I know..." I said.

"And?" Irene asked. "How do you feel about him?"

Not for the first time, I thought about telling her about Roger still being alive. How could I explain any of it, though, without giving away more than I was allowed to?

"I...just don't know," I said. "I didn't think I would ever have to love anyone else. The idea of it is just..."

"Too much, and perhaps too soon," Irene said, laying

a hand on my shoulder. "That's quite all right, dear. You should only ever accept if you feel it is the right time. But who knows? Maybe you would enjoy having dinner with him." Her lips curled into a mischievous smile.

I smirked at her. "Not biased at all, are you?"

"I only want what's best for you, my dear," she said, her smile warm and gentle.

"I'm sorry, what is it that you needed?" I asked. "Here we are, talking about me..."

"Oh, of course," Irene said. "Nathanial and I decided to throw a little impromptu get together this evening for his brother who has come in from out of town. We were wondering if you would like to join us."

"Oh, I'd love to," I said. "That would be the perfect way to get all this stuff with Sam off my mind..."

2

The get together at the Driscoll's ended up being a great deal more fun than I had anticipated it would be. After sending Michael over to Irene's parents' house for the night, we spent the evening playing board games, eating Irene's delicious treats, and enjoying good conversations with great company.

Nathanial's brother, Ralph, was quite the comedian. He had a terribly dry sense of humor, but seemed all too happy to make sure people laughed and had a good time. When Irene asked why he hadn't yet found anyone, Ralph threw back his head and laughed. "Do you really think anyone would be able to handle me, dear sister? I would drive the poor woman batty before the end of our first week of marriage."

His eyes, the same shade of blue as his brother's, turned to me.

"And why is your friend here also alone?" Ralph asked. "Someone as lovely as she is must surely be the sort of woman that all men dream about."

I blushed.

"Actually, she may not be alone for very long," Irene said, winking at me.

"What do you mean by that?" Nathanial asked, sitting up straighter in his chair.

Irene's smirk grew. "The good Inspector has asked Irene out for dinner with him."

Nathanial's jaw dropped.

"Well, it seems I was just too late, then," Ralph said with a wink at me. "Better luck next time, I suppose."

"That is, if I choose to accept," I said.

"He's a good man, Helen," Nathanial said, nodding firmly. "He would take care of you, no doubt about that."

"He certainly would," Irene said. "I think he'd be frightened to let you out of his sight for even a minute. Not that I blame him, of course. You do tend to get yourself into trouble every time you turn around."

"Trouble?" Ralph asked. "How very interesting. What sort of trouble?"

"Not the sort of trouble that you need to know anything about," Nathanial said, laughing. "Come on, Ralph. Let's go check on those chops."

I appreciated their concern for me, and knew that if Roger had never revealed himself, I certainly would have considered their opinions more seriously on the matter. Irene must have certainly been confused that I wasn't enticed by the idea as much as I might have been before, but she still didn't know the truth...

I knew eventually she would ask me why I wasn't willing to accept Sam's offer. And how could I lie to Irene? She would be able to see right through me. And I felt horribly guilty about it all.

I would have to worry about that when the time came.

Nathanial and Irene walked me back home that night, well after ten o'clock. The moon was bright and full, the stars peppered across the sky like flecks of diamonds scattered across the velvety expanse.

"You know, I think Sam would be a good match for you," Nathanial said. "I really do. If I were you, I would seriously consider it. He's a reliable fellow. Not like that Sidney Mason..."

"He is reliable," I said. "I know he is. And he and I are quite good friends by now. He would certainly try to make me very happy. I suppose I wish I had met him under different circumstances, is all."

Nathanial opened his mouth to say more, but Irene laid a hand on his arm. "She only just lost her husband this past March, dear. That is not something one should rush to get over so quickly."

Nathanial's face became sheepish. "You're right. I'm sorry, Helen. I didn't mean to push you."

"It's all right," I said, smiling at him. "I appreciate how much you both care about me. You really have been so wonderful to me since I moved here...I don't know what I would do without you both."

After a somewhat weepy goodbye, I settled into my house, appreciating it for all its coziness and security, and was fast asleep before I saw midnight on the clock on my side table.

THE NEXT MORNING seemed to come as soon as I closed

my eyes. The next thing I knew, the sunlight was streaming in through the window above my bed.

I sat up slowly, stretching my arms up over my head, inhaling the cool, morning air.

I glanced over at the clock. Just after six. Perfect. I had enough time to get ready before the shop opened.

I took a leisurely shower, enjoying the warmth of the water on my shoulders, which were somewhat sore from the tension of my conversation with Sam the night before. Thinking about it once again, I found the guilt returning as I feared telling him that I was not interested in pursuing a personal relationship any further with him. Would it hurt him? Would he be angry with me?

And then what if Roger ever came back, revealing himself perhaps as someone else? What if we had to keep up a rouse for others to see?

All in all, I didn't want to hurt Sam's feelings. I wanted to remain friends with him, without any uncomfortable distance being created between us.

He was a strong man, and he did tell me it was my decision. I had to believe he was mature enough to accept my answer, even if it was the one he wouldn't want to hear.

More than anything, I worried what Roger might think if he were to discover I had gone out with another man, especially now knowing he was still alive. Before I had known, it might have made sense.

It made me wonder how much it might have hurt him to see me leave the house that day, all dressed up and done up? Did he know where I was headed?

I wondered if he'd followed me, curious about where I was going. I wondered if he'd been shocked to see me meeting a man, and only a man, at the inn where Sam and I enjoyed lunch together.

I knew it would have broken my heart to see him with another woman somewhere, even if he had no idea I was still alive...

No, I was going to have to let Sam know that I couldn't step out with him...not as anything more than just friends.

I dried my hair and brushed it through, like I did every morning. I ran some hair oil that Irene swore by through my hair, enjoying the pleasant, flowery smell that it gave off, feeling as if I was using something rather expensive and luxurious.

Lipstick, mascara, and the lightest touch of blush across my cheekbones...and I was ready for the day.

I wandered to my kitchen, prepared myself some tea and a light breakfast of a hardboiled egg with a slice of bread I'd baked the morning before, slathered in a delicious cheese from the party at Irene's the other night.

The shop itself was still and quiet as I prepared for the day, though I felt it needed something. Perhaps some of the flowers growing out in my back garden, the last that would likely bloom before the spring?

I picked a dozen or so mums in brightest red, carrying them inside as I hummed softly to myself. I filled a pale blue, milk glass jar that had once belonged to my aunt with cold water from the tap in the washroom downstairs, and set the mums inside, admiring their beauty and delicate scent.

I set them down beside the till, smiling at them. Perhaps they would brighten someone's day the same way they had brightened mine.

The shop opened a short while later. Mrs. Georgianna, a frequent and loyal customer, appeared shortly after I'd flipped the sign on the front door. "Oh, dear, I'm just terribly eager to see these new threads you have," she said. "Spun silk? How wonderful."

I led her to the cabinet I'd chosen for the threads, the many small drawers previously being used for extra ribbons and buttons I'd accumulated that had no pairs or home.

"And what lovely flowers," Mrs. Georgianna said, gazing at the bright red pop of color near the back of the shop. "I just love mums. A wonderful reflection of autumn, aren't they?"

"They certainly are," I said. "I couldn't resist bringing some cheer into the shop today."

"Oh, how very wise of you," Mrs. Georgianna said. "I'm certain there will be many who will appreciate it."

I smiled at her as I made my way back over to the wooden box of glass jars where I kept the more expensive glass beads, all organized by color and size. I'd noticed a few of the reds had been mixed in with the greens, and so set about reorganizing them for the next guests who might want them.

I adjusted the box as Mrs. Georgianna happily looked through the new stock of threads I'd purchased, and the sound of the bell at the door made me look up.

Mrs. Trent and Mrs. Henrietta strolled inside, their heads bent low, both speaking in low voices.

"Good morning, ladies," I said, making my way over to them. "Is there anything I can help you find?"

Mrs. Trent looked up at me. "Oh, yes, well, I was

wondering if I could place an order for a dress of mine to be hemmed and resized."

"Of course," I said. "Just come back here and I'll take your measurements."

The two women followed me back to a corner where a three-paneled mirror stood behind a low dais. I picked up a measuring tape from the wall as Mrs. Trent stepped up onto it.

"Now, it's a red dress," she said. "And it is just far too short for me to be comfortable. I don't know what I did to it, trying to take it in."

"That's no trouble at all," I said. "I might even be able to match the fabric if I see it."

"Very good," Mrs. Trent said, frowning at her own reflection.

I caught a glimpse of Mrs. Henrietta in the mirror, as she dabbed at her eyes with a handkerchief. While I knelt down beside Mrs. Trent to take the measurements from her hip to her ankle, I looked over at the real Mrs. Henrietta. "Is everything all right, Mrs. Henrietta?"

"Oh, I suppose I'll be all right," she said, sniffling. "Though it's quite hard to believe what happened, isn't it? Especially after running into him last night the way we did."

A knot began to form in my chest, and somewhere deep down inside, something suddenly felt...wrong. "Quite hard to believe that what happened, exactly?" I asked, jotting down Mrs. Trent's measurements onto a pad of paper.

Mrs. Henrietta looked over at Mrs. Trent, whose eyes widened. "You...didn't hear?" she asked.

It was as if I'd swallowed a rock. "Didn't hear what?" I asked.

"It was in the papers this morning," she said. "Front page and everything…"

"What was?" I asked, getting to my feet, my heart beginning to thunder loudly in my ears, the fear already beginning to snake its way through my arms and legs, making my knees weak.

"Inspector Graves, my dear," Mrs. Henrietta said tearfully. "He died last night."

The measuring tape fell from between my fingers, bouncing off the floor before coiling into a knotted mess beneath a chair behind me. "He…he what?" I asked, breathless.

"It happened sometime last night," Mrs. Trent said. "In the alleyway behind Mr. Hodgins' butcher shop."

My head pounded. This couldn't be true. It just…it couldn't be.

I collapsed in the chair behind me, my insides filling with icy numbness.

"How…I don't understand," I said, feeling as if something large and heavy was compressing my chest. "He – I just saw him, last night. He was here, at my house, and I –"

"I know, dear, I know," Mrs. Henrietta said, coming over to me and laying a hand on my shoulder. "It's all right. Just take deep breaths. You cannot allow yourself to panic."

My mind raced. It wasn't possible. He couldn't have died. Not when I had seen him only twelve hours ago. Or was it fourteen now?

"Lydia, be a dear and go get some cold water," Mrs.

Henrietta said, kneeling down beside me. "There, now, dear, come now and try to remember to breathe."

I couldn't think of anything except Sam.

A moment or two later, a cold glass was pressed into my hand, and Mrs. Henrietta was doing her best to encourage me to drink it. I wanted nothing to do with it, of course. "Bring me the paper," I said. "Out on the front step. Please."

"She's in too much distress right now," Mrs. Henrietta said. "She needs rest, and perhaps to see a doctor – "

"No!" I said. "Bring me the paper. Please."

Mrs. Trent gave Mrs. Henrietta a troubled look before rising to feet and heading back toward the door.

"Good heavens, is everything all right?"

It was Mrs. Georgianna, only just now catching onto what was happening at the back of the store.

"Yes, I believe so," Mrs. Henrietta said. "I think she's just a little shaken about the news of Inspector Graves' death."

Mrs. Georgianna suppressed a shiver. "Oh, most troubling indeed. I don't even understand how it happened. How could someone have managed to kill him, as trained and as skilled as he was?"

"Killed him?" I asked, another surge of paralyzing fear shooting through my veins. "He was killed?"

"Yes, dear, rather brutally too, from what the paper said," Mrs. Georgianna said, shaking her head. "Stabbed to death, or some such terrible thing – "

The breath itself seemed to be stolen right from my lungs. I grasped at my chest, unable to draw a full breath.

"Mrs. Georgianna, if you would be so kind as to call

for a doctor," Mrs. Henrietta said, rather forcefully. "That would be much appreciated."

Mrs. Georgianna hurried away to find a phone and do just that.

Sam Graves...murdered? How could it even happen? Who would dare to do such a terrible thing?

"A doctor is on his way," Mrs. Georgianna said a few minutes later, returning to my side. "Can I do anything else?"

"Perhaps give the poor girl some space," Mrs. Henrietta said.

Mrs. Trent appeared as well, the newspaper rolled up in her hands. She gave me a very serious look, which I was only partially aware of. "Are you certain you want to read this? I know how close the two of you were..."

I swallowed, or at least attempted to, my mouth having long since gone dry. "I...yes," I said. "Yes, please."

She passed it to me.

Just as I was about to unfold it, the phone on the wall behind me rang.

I sprang from my seat, wheeling around to look at it.

"It's all right dear, you don't have to answer," Mrs. Henrietta said.

"I need to," I said, a million hopes running through my mind. Perhaps the paper was wrong. Perhaps he was still alive, and was calling to ensure I knew he was all right. Perhaps it was Roger, somehow calling to comfort me in my loss.

I ran to the telephone, ignoring the warnings from the women behind me, my legs wobbling as I struggled to put weight on them.

"Hello?" I asked, breathless as I picked up the receiver.

"Helen?" It was Irene. "Oh, Helen...I...I don't even know what to say..."

My heart plummeted to the floor beneath me. "Irene..." I said. "Sam – "

Irene burst into tears on the other end of the phone. "I am so sorry, dear," she said. "After everything we talked about last night...after seeing him, and interrupting him...if maybe he had stayed with you, talked with you some more, maybe things wouldn't have worked out the way they did – "

My eyes stung, and my bottom lip trembled. "Irene, we – we can't think like that," I said, trying to keep my emotions in check. "There isn't anything we could have – "

But was there? Could I have done something to prevent this?

What if she was right? What if I had agreed to go out with him? Would we have gone to dinner last night? Perhaps lingered there at the restaurant, enjoying our conversation? Would it have saved his life?

Tears splashed down onto my cheeks, and my legs gave way beneath me.

Arms wrapped around me a moment later as Irene and I cried on the phone together, mumbling indistinguishable reassurances to one another, each trying to comfort the other. Somehow, I was helped to my feet and replaced into another chair.

"I'm coming down there," Irene said. "You – you shouldn't be alone."

I just nodded, unable to contain the sadness any longer.

I wasn't sure who it was that took the receiver out of my hand and finished the conversation with Irene for me. I continued to cry into my hands, no longer able to find the strength to resist the tidal wave of sorrow that was crashing against my soul.

This wasn't just someone I'd never met. This wasn't a long lost relative, or a victim of war, or even someone who vaguely reminded me of myself.

It had hurt me when Mr. James died, especially when I felt like there was more I could have done to help him, feeling almost responsible for his death in the first place. But this....this was something entirely different.

This was almost like finding out Roger was gone.

Somewhere in the back of my mind, buried beneath the layers of sadness and disbelief, I began to formulate a plan. Anger seeped into my heart, a thirst for revenge that I had never known.

I was going to find out who had killed Sam, just like I did what I could to find out who had supposedly killed Roger. This was not going to go unanswered.

I would have no help. I knew that I would not receive the support from the police I had become somewhat dependent upon.

Nevertheless, I was determined to find out who killed him...and I was going to do all I could to make sure they got the punishment they deserved.

3

The thirst for revenge, it turned out, was an ugly emotion. Like poison, it seeped into my every thought, coating every aspect of my life until it was as if I had never thought of anything else, and could think of nothing else.

Irene was the one who pointed it out later that day.

She and I sat up in my flat, the shop having long since been closed, on our third pot of tea for the afternoon.

"This is unhealthy, you know..." she said. "If you aren't careful, you're sure to become obsessed with finding out who did this."

"Would you rather whoever it was get away with it?" I asked.

"No," Irene said firmly. "But this is *not* your responsibility. Even if you were close with him, it doesn't mean that you need to be the one to avenge him."

The shock had worn off slightly, and I'd taken the time to read the article about Sam's death. Irene had pleaded with me not to, insisting that she give me the summary, knowing it would be better coming from a friend. I had refused, naturally, knowing she might leave vital information out in order to spare my feelings, as kind as she thought that might be.

"What I don't understand is how no one else witnessed it," I said. "Especially given the proximity to so many homes and businesses. Not only is the butcher's shop right there, but families live in those homes surrounding it."

"It happened so late, though. Everyone could have been sleeping. Or it could have happened so fast that no one would have been able to hear it in the first place," Irene said, her nose wrinkling even as she said the words. "Goodness, I hate even thinking about it like that…"

"I should go and look in the alleyway," I said. "See if the killer left behind any clue as to his identity."

"You cannot be serious," Irene said. "This really should be left to the police, you know that – "

"And what if they do nothing?" I asked. "What if this whole thing goes completely unresolved?"

"Helen, listen to yourself," Irene said, setting her teacup down and glaring at me. "Do you really think that the police would let something like this go? When there is so much at stake? One of their own men was killed. If anything, that fact alone will push them to solve this crime so they can maintain good standing in the community."

I frowned, ceasing my pacing back and forth across the room for just a moment. She had a point.

"As it is, everyone is frightened. The Inspector, a man everyone respected and trusted, is gone. To everyone else, it proves that no one in Brookminster is safe. Not even a man whose entire job is to represent safety."

Right again. "But what I don't understand is...who reported the murder?" I asked. "Who was the one who found him dead?"

"The article doesn't say," Irene said, folding her arms. "It must have been someone that lived nearby."

"Maybe they saw something else, too..." I said. "I'm sorry, Irene, I know you don't want me to go, but Sam would have trusted me with something like this if he was still – " I couldn't bring myself to finish the sentence. "He would have trusted me to do this for him."

Irene shook her head. "You will never learn, will you? It doesn't matter what I say, or what I do...you are going to do what you want to anyway, aren't you?"

"I'm sorry," I said. "I just...I can't leave this be."

Irene studied my face for a long, hard moment. "You cared about him. So did we all. I just hope you really know what you are doing, and aren't letting your emotions govern your actions."

Normally, I would have agreed with her. But in that moment, I thought it was a very good thing that my emotions were the ones to drive me to do what I was going to.

I made my way before it became too dark down to the alleyway where the paper had said Sam had been killed.

Killed...it's still hard to even think that, I thought. *He was the last person I ever would have expected to meet such a terrible fate.*

I'd been back here before, when the body of the Polish beggar had been found in Mr. Englewood's shed, in the alleyway between his home and the butcher's shop.

It felt strange, making my way back here once again to investigate another death...

I walked past the shed, finding myself in the long stretch of alley, the shadows of several homes pressing in on one another. Most of them had barely any room for more than a few meters of grass in their back gardens before they joined with the path separating them.

My knees shook as I peered around. Nothing seemed entirely out of order. There weren't any distinguishing scuffs in the dirt path beneath my feet, though I wondered if any of the smudges or indents could have been footprints that had been trampled by the police when they had come to investigate.

Rubbish bins stood against the back of almost all of the homes. Shovels leaned up against the walls, and coils of rope and hoses were scattered around. Bags of fertilizer were stacked behind Mr. Englewood's home, along with a few freshly painted terracotta planters. I wondered what they intended to plant before the first frosts came.

All of the homes surrounding the alleyway also had windows looking into the back gardens. Drapes were pulled on every one of them, likely due to the time of day. Any number of eyes could have witnessed what happened. Why hadn't they reported it to the police? Or was that how Sam's body had been discovered? Someone had thrown open their drapes in the morning only to find a prostrate man lying in the dirt?

My stomach twisted as I examined the pathway a little more closely. With every passing beat of my heart, I was certain that I would see blood mixed in with the dirt and stones on the ground. I never found any, though. The police must have done what they could to cover it up... something I was thoroughly grateful for.

I swallowed hard, looking around at all the houses once again.

I supposed the best place to start would just be to speak with the residents of the homes around, see what they might have witnessed.

Then maybe I could –

I stopped in my tracks, my mind buzzing as I realized that the last half of that thought was no longer possible. Without thinking, I had been making plans to go see Sam, to tell him what I'd learned, to see if he could do any further investigating...

And then it hit me all over again that I was investigating *his* murder, *his* death...and my already delicately patched together heart shattered once again.

I shook my head, and made my way back through the alleyway to the main street, where I walked up to Mr. Englewood's door and knocked.

He appeared a few moments later, dressed in a nightcap and silk gown that was tied around his waist. "Mrs. Lightholder," he said, squinting as he adjusted his glasses on his crooked nose. "My apologies for not being in any condition to receive you, but I wasn't expecting company."

"No, that's all right, Mr. Englewood," I said. "I was just stopping by to ask you a couple of questions."

"Well...all right," Mr. Englewood said, his wispy eyebrows furrowing together. "You look rather distressed. Is everything all right?"

"I'm not quite sure," I said.

I glanced over my shoulder, up the street, hoping against all hope that we would not be overheard.

"Mr. Englewood, I know this may be unpleasant for you to discuss, but...did you witness anything strange last night? Out in the alleyway behind your house?" I asked.

The wrinkles on Mr. Englewood's forehead deepened, and he looked down at his slippered feet. "You mean to discuss what happened to the Inspector?" he asked, nodding, smacking his lips. "Yes, I suppose you would, given that you were friends...No, I didn't see or hear anything, and to me, that's the strangest part of it all. I was awake for most of the night reading last night, and I heard no more than the wind against the shutters and the occasional hoot of an owl. It's deeply troubling to me that something so horrendous happened right outside my back garden, and I was none the wiser until this very morning..." He looked up at me, the color having been leeched from his face. "It's quite troubling when this isn't the first murder to occur so very near to my home."

I knew he was referring to the Polish beggar, who was found dead in the shed between his home and the butcher's.

"But you were not home the first time, Mr. Englewood," I reassured him. "No one blames you for what happened with the beggar."

"Nevertheless..." Mr. Englewood said. "I am still shaken about what happened to Inspector Graves. To have been killed in such a terrible way..."

My throat grew tight, and the bile rose from my stomach. But I still had to ask. "Mr. Englewood, do you know who it was that found him out there?" I asked.

Mr. Englewood shook his head. "Good heavens, no... but I am certainly glad it was not I who did."

I could understand his relief. "What about any of the other homes in the alley?" I asked. "Do you think any of your neighbors saw anything?"

"Well, I can't be certain of that..." he said, looking over my shoulder. "For one, I know the Mayfields left in the early evening yesterday. They weren't even here when this all happened."

"Which house is theirs?" I asked.

"The one directly behind mine," he said. "And then there's the butcher, and then across from their home, the Gallette's, and I know for certain they didn't see anything either, as I spoke to them this morning after reading the paper. They were just as surprised as I was..."

How had such a murder occurred? And what was Sam doing back there in that alley in the first place?

"I'm sorry I don't have more information for you," he said. "These were all the same questions the police asked me earlier. I wish I could have been more helpful."

"You were very helpful," I said. "I suppose I should go ask the Hodgins if they saw or heard anything."

"Perhaps they did," he said. "Though I can't imagine they were up as late as that, given their young family."

"My thoughts exactly," I said. "Thank you for your time, Mr. Englewood."

"It was my pleasure, Mrs. Lightholder. I certainly hope they are able to find who did this...."

"So do I," I said.

I bid him goodnight and made my way over to the Gallette's home. It wasn't that I didn't trust Mr. Englewood, but it was better to hear it from their mouths.

Just like Mr. Englewood said, they knew nothing about what had occurred the night before. "Everything was quiet, as far as we knew," Mr. Gallette said. "Nothing out of the ordinary...or so we thought."

"I'm not certain I will ever let the boys back out there to play again," Mrs. Gallette said, pulling the shrug she wore more closely around herself. "Knowing such a terrible thing occurred back there. What if the killer comes back?"

That was my fear, too, and I worried that it was someone who would walk through there, and no one would even notice.

These fears kept the nervousness flooding through me as I said goodnight to the Gallette's, wondering if I would ever find the answers I sought.

I sighed heavily, looking back down into the alleyway.

"Only one more place to check," I said. "I wonder if Mr. Hodgins saw anything unusual..."

I made my way through the growing darkness, toward the butcher shop, my heart in my throat. Why couldn't this have been someone else? Why did it have to be Sam Graves, the one man that I needed to solve all of this?

4

I made my way back into the alleyway, paying close attention to all my surroundings.

It was difficult to see clearly, as night had begun to fall, and the shadows were growing in length and depth, their darkness filling every corner and angle like ink, fluid and malleable. The alleyway smelled of damp earth and smoke, the fireplaces of the surrounding houses spewing the billowing air high up into the sky overhead. Aside from my own footsteps, there were no sounds that seemed out of place; a woman sang out her open window half a dozen houses down the row, and a dog barked somewhere near the front of Mr. Englewood's home.

I noticed the house directly behind Mr. Englewood's, the house that belonged to the Mayfield's. It was quiet, as one might expect when the occupants were out of town. All the windows remained dark, and yet something seemed to glint in the light trickling down the alley from the lamp hanging over the back door of the butcher's shop.

As I drew nearer, I squinted up at it. Had they forgotten to shut off a small lamp before departing? Or perhaps, and a much worse thought, they forgot to put a candle out?

When I was standing behind it, however, I realized that it was not a light, nor a candle...but a reflection.

A reflection on jagged, broken glass.

One of the windows, too high to reach from the ground, had been broken.

"How awful..." I thought, peering up at it. "And just as soon as the Mayfield's left on their trip..."

That wasn't entirely uncommon, though, I knew. Roger had witnessed something similar back when we were recently married.

He'd come home from work, and with a heavy sigh, told me that our neighbor's home had been broken into.

"Why?" I'd asked. "What happened?"

Roger shrugged. "It doesn't surprise me much," he said. "Not when they were telling everyone in town they were going to be gone for three weeks. That's essentially alerting everyone to the fact that there will be a vacant house, likely with valuables inside."

"How terrible," I said, frowning at him. "How could someone rob their neighbors?"

"People aren't always as kind as you are, my love," he said. "Though I certainly wish they were."

That memory, as clear as crystal, faded from my mind as I stared up at the broken window.

*It must be exactly the same thing...*I thought. *Someone*

knew the Mayfield's were leaving, and decided to take it as an opportunity to break into their house. What a shame...

There were now two mysteries on hand. Sam's murder, and the potential robbery of the Mayfield's home.

Was it possible the broken window was somehow tied to Sam's death? Had the two events occurred simultaneously?

I made note of it in my mind, and continued on down toward the butcher's, just to see if anyone there had witnessed anything strange.

I walked through the narrow alley between the butcher's and Mr. Englewood's home, and walked up to the front door, where I knocked as loud as I could.

I stood outside for a long moment, with no answer.

A car drove past behind me, and the dog I'd heard barking earlier began its frantic yelping once again as the car continued on down the street.

I decided to knock again. *If they aren't home tonight, I suppose I can always come back tomorrow.*

I knocked, and stepped back to wait once again.

The response was much shorter than I expected, perhaps nothing more than a heartbeat or two.

A young man wearing an apron and black rubber gloves answered the door. It wasn't Mr. Hodgins' son, who I'd seen working there nearly every time I had gone into the shop. He looked vaguely familiar, though. Tall, lean, with clear blue eyes and the first signs of stubble along his jawline. He couldn't have been older than nineteen, perhaps twenty.

"Can I help you?" he asked in a voice that demonstrated the least amount of friendliness possible.

"Um, yes," I said. "I was looking for Mr. Hodgins, is he here?"

"No," said the young man. "I'm closing up for him tonight."

"Oh, I see," I said. "I don't think we've met yet. You must be new to the shop."

"In a way," the young man said, pinching the end of the finger of one of his gloves, loosening it, and then moving to the next. "I used to work here before I was shipped off to boarding school. I just got back this summer, and my mother insisted I find a job."

"So Mr. Hodgins hired you on again?" I asked.

"I thought that would be obvious," the young man said.

"Well, my name is Helen Lightholder, and I – "

"I'm Arthur Barnes," he said. "It's nice to meet you, but I – "

"Oh, you're Victoria's son?" I asked. "I've heard so much about you. Your mother comes into my haberdashery every two weeks. I've likely mended the buttons on your school uniform at one time or another."

He gave me a stiff smile. "Have you now?" he asked. He pulled one glove free, and used his clean hand to unroll the other glove from his still sheathed arm. "How wonderful." His tone told me it was the least wonderful thing he could think of.

"Well, I certainly won't trouble you for long, Mr. Barnes," I said. "I simply had some questions for Mr. Hodgins about the murder that happened out here in the alleyway last night."

Arthur's eyes widened with interest. "What about it?" he asked.

"I was wondering if Mr. Hodgins heard anything about it," I said. "If anything strange had happened last night."

He finished pulling the glove off the other hand, revealing a thick bandage wrapped around his palm.

"That's a rather nasty wound," I said, eyeing his hand. "How did it happen?"

"Oh, this?" he asked. "I suppose you can't work in a butcher's shop for long without running into an accident with one of the knives. And to answer your question, nothing strange that I know," he said. "We were in here finishing dividing up some cattle that came in late yesterday. I'm not even certain how long we were here."

"I see," I said.

He folded his arms, tucking his injured hand underneath. "Are you working with the police?" he asked.

"I used to," I said. "Sam Graves – Inspector Graves, and I, were good friends. I did some work with him, consulting work, and helped him to investigate some of the crimes happening around the village."

"Yes, I've heard," Arthur said. "My mother told me there was someone who seemed to be quite the sleuth. Are you the woman who just moved into town this past March?"

"Yes, that's me," I said.

"Well, Brookminster is certainly lucky to have you," he said, that stiff smile returning. "Now, I hate to be rude, but – "

"I'm sure you must be busy, trying to close for the night, but I did have one more question," I said. "I noticed that the Mayfield's are not here. Their house seems rather dark, and I was speaking with Mr. and Mrs. Henrietta last night, and they told me they just left on a trip to see their son. When I was walking past their house this evening, I noticed that one of their windows was broken, up on the second floor."

"Is it?" he asked, glancing past me out into the dark alleyway, his eyes narrowing. "Well, that's certainly unfortunate for them, isn't it?"

"Yes, most unfortunate," I said. "You didn't hear the sound of glass breaking? Or anything like that?" I asked.

He shook his head. "No. Our heads were buried in the freezer for most of the night. Can hardly hear a thing in there."

"Right, of course," I said.

This conversation was getting me nowhere. He seemed either entirely indifferent to my questions, or simply couldn't be bothered to answer them for me.

Still, I was interrupting him while he was attempting to close the shop, and I knew that Mr. Hodgins would likely be upset if he learned I was holding the boy up from finishing his duties.

"Take care of that wound on your hand, all right?" I asked. "I'm sure you've learned this, but those knives are dangerous."

"Oh, yes, they certainly are," he said. "And thank you. I will keep that in mind. Thanks for stopping by. I'll make sure to tell Mr. Hodgins that you did."

"Thank you, I appreciate it," I said.

With that, I turned and walked away from the front of the shop, making my way back across the now dark street, where the puddles of light from the street lamps were flooding the road.

No new answers had been uncovered, and I found myself distinctly distressed by this. How on earth was I going to solve a crime if there were no clues to follow?

From stepping back into that alleyway, I could have assumed that nothing had occurred back there. Aside from the broken window, there were absolutely no clues in the first place. No blood, no weapons, no scuffs in the wall or on the ground.

And how was it that a man had been murdered in that alley, and no one had heard it happen? Neither the murder, nor the window breaking? How were there no witnesses to any of these events?

Either the killer somehow managed to attack Sam without him seeing it coming or having the chance to make a sound...or someone was lying.

I pondered over these ideas as I walked home, others in town starting to make their way back through the village as well, likely longing for the rest their beds provided.

Well...even if the alleyway held no answers, I do wonder about the window at the Mayfield's...Someone should be alerted to the break-in, as that certainly will not be a pleasant surprise to return home to.

I was inclined to believe Mr. Englewood. Who wouldn't, after he had already dealt with the discovery of the poor Polish beggar's body in his shed just a few months before? He seemed distressed about the Inspector's death, wishing he had been able to help in some way.

The Gallette's were the same. Unable to help, none the wiser until they met with Mr. Englewood this very morning. And their stories matched, which was always a good indication that they were telling the truth.

I did wonder what Mr. Hodgins had seen, and wished he'd been there instead of his impatient assistant. I debated about reaching out the next day and trying to speak with him again.

Though, given he was one of the people who seemed so certain I was responsible for killing Mr. James, perhaps he won't be so willing to speak with me. Perhaps it was advantageous that I was able to speak with his assistant, as unfriendly as he was.

I unlocked the front door of my home, staring briefly upward toward the higher windows, ensuring they were all still intact. I wasn't sure why anyone would dare to break my windows, but it certainly made me curious as to why no one seemed to disturb my home when I went away to London both those times.

I thought of Sam, in that moment, knowing that he had likely been watching over the house, along with Irene, and even Sidney...though Sidney had been the one who had been breaking into my house to steal things relating to Roger...

It was quite troubling to think that two people I'd cared about had been taken away from me now. Three, if I included the man I believed Sidney to be. Two by death, and one by deceit. Was it possible to mourn the loss of a friend that never really even existed?

I wished Roger could be with me now, helping me to cope with the loss of another friend.

He can't be, at least not right now, I thought. *I need to solve this crime on my own. It's what Sam would have expected me to do. He's counting on me to set things right.*

I knew he would have done as much, in my place. And that gave me the determination to continue moving forward.

5

I knew one of the first moves I had to make was to let the police know about the window at the Mayfield's home. Even if they didn't know about the fact that I had been back there to look for clues about Sam, they still needed to know that someone had broken into one of the residents' homes.

What a wonderful thing for us. First a murderer, but now also a thief.

I was beginning to wonder if all little villages had these sorts of people residing in them, or if it was just Brookminster.

"That's how people are, Helen," I heard Sam's voice say to me. *"I know we all want to believe there is some good in everyone, that it's possible for us to get along...but in all my years of serving on the police force, I have seen just the opposite. The worst of the worst. The sort of behavior you would never imagine people capable of, and yet they are."*

"But that's an awfully cynical view on life, Sam," I mumbled as I brushed my hair, readying myself for bed.

"It might be, but at least it's the truth, and the truth is the truth, no matter how you feel about it."

I stared at my reflection.

The truth was the truth, no matter how I felt about it.

The truth I was faced with now was that Sam was gone. He'd been killed. That meant someone was responsible for it, someone had raised a hand to him, and intentionally made the choice to take his life.

The truth was that I had yet to find any clues, and had no idea where to even begin looking for them.

The truth was that I needed help, and there was really only one place that I was going to be able to get the help I needed.

The police.

I SAT in front of the phone the next morning for nearly ten minutes, contemplating how I was going to make the call. I knew if anyone in the reception area knew it was me calling, they would either deny me the chance to speak to anyone, or they would possibly chastise me. Especially Rachel, who I thought might even go as far as to try and tie me to Sam's death, given our close friendship.

It surprised me, actually, that I had not yet been questioned by anyone.

Not yet been questioned. I supposed that was the operative thought.

I remembered Sam mentioning some names on the force that he would have considered friends, people he would have trusted above all others. I did my best to recall exactly what those names were.

The chief was a good man, though he followed the rulebook to the letter, and likely would not appreciate my call, even for something to do with Sam's murder, or something that could be tied to it.

I thought of Richard Doss, who was another one of the officers Sam talked about. Sam said he had a great deal of promise, but due to his lower position in the station, he likely wouldn't be able to give me the sort of help I was looking for.

One more name flickered across my memory. Sergeant Newton. Another man like the chief, who wouldn't budge an inch on the law, even for those he cared about, Sam always spoke about him with utmost respect. They never had the chance to work together, though, as the chief always put them on different cases at different times. Half the time, Sergeant Newton wasn't even in Brookminster, and instead was working with another Inspector in the next town over.

He was likely going to be my best bet. The one person who might actually listen to me for more than a moment as I attempted to communicate about what I'd found.

I dialed the number of the police station, and waited patiently for someone to pick up.

"Brookminster Police, what is your emergency?"

It was Rachel. I recognized her voice immediately.

"No emergency, but I am looking for Sergeant Newton," I said. "And it is rather important."

"Important, you say?" Rachel asked in her nasally voice. "I'm sorry, but the Sergeant is very busy, and has asked not to be distur – "

"I'm sorry, but every time I call, it seems that whoever it is that I am looking to speak with, they are *very busy* and have asked not to be disturbed," I said, my patience thinning far faster than I had expected it to. "I very much doubt that there isn't a moment that he could spare to speak with someone who might have information for him about Inspector Graves' murder?"

There was silence on the other end of the line, and the only sounds I heard were the ringing of phones and the chatter of conversation from somewhere around her.

"One moment please," she said, a bite to her words, but I didn't care.

There was a distinct click on the other end, and for a moment, all I heard was the sound of my own breathing, which was faster than it should have been. My heart began to beat more quickly, my face flushing pink.

Did I really have sufficient grounds to be calling the police? It wasn't like calling Sam, where he was familiar enough with me to know that I likely had something concrete that was worth discussing. Would this sergeant simply think I was wasting his time?

"Sergeant Newton," came the voice on the other line. Deep, yet not as deep as Sam's had been.

It was so sudden, and I had been so lost in my own thoughts, that his voice made me jump.

"Good morning, Sergeant," I said, trying my best to regain my composure. "My name is Helen Lightholder, and – "

"Mrs. Lightholder," Sergeant Newton said. I recognized the tiredness in his voice. "I expected to hear from you before long. Graves told me that you had a way of always sticking your nose into these cases, and here you are, right on time."

My brow furrowed. I wasn't sure if he was being serious or not, and that annoyed me.

"What can I do for you? What information have you uncovered that we, as police officers, have somehow missed?" he asked.

"Pardon me, sir, but I do not appreciate the chastisement," I said. "Inspector Graves was a dear friend, and I don't like the tone you are using to speak about him – "

"My apologies, Mrs. Lightholder, I meant no harm by it," he said. "I am deeply saddened by his loss, do not doubt me." I heard him shifting in his chair, the wood creaking as he moved. The change in his voice made the knots around my heart ease somewhat. "In regards to the investigation, I do not mean to sound harsh, but this really is a matter that should be handled by the police, and the police alone." He paused a moment before adding, "That being said, I trust my friend Sam, and something about you got him to trust you. I have only ever seen that happen one other time. His trust was hard earned. Because of that I'm willing to hear you out this once, and then ask that you leave the rest of the investigation to us. I could have contacted you for questioning about his death, given your relationship, but I didn't think it necessary. I didn't need to do that in order to know you weren't involved."

"Well..." I said, a mixture of emotions flooding through me. "I appreciate your faith in me, but isn't that showing favoritism?"

"Not when I've been working for the police as long as

I have been," he said. "You just get a feel about some people, understand how their minds work."

I remembered Sam saying something similar.

"Would you rather me bring you in to question?" he asked.

"Well, no," I said.

"Good," he said. "And I doubt you were calling to admit you committed the crime?"

"Of course not," I said, my brow furrowing, my hand balling into a fist.

"That's what I thought," he said. "Now, what was the real reason you called?"

I fidgeted, feeling rather flustered. It was as if he chased me around like a fox chasing a rabbit. I couldn't quite decide if he was attempting to be friendly or distant, or perhaps a mixture of both.

Could I trust him? Just because he trusted Sam, and he said Sam made it clear that he trusted me, did that mean he was trustworthy?

My head throbbed, and I rubbed my temple. "I saw something last night that troubled me," I said. "While I was out visiting the butcher's, I glanced up at the Mayfield's home, knowing they were out of town, and noticed one of their windows had been broken."

"Broken, you say?" he asked. "That's odd. I wonder if it occurred before they left on their trip."

"I don't know," I said. "I asked Mr. Hodgin's assistant, Arthur Barnes, and he said he had no idea what had happened. It just seemed rather strange that there was a broken window so very near to where...well, where Sam was attacked."

The chair creaked on the other line once again. "It was in the alleyway, you say?" he asked.

"It was at the back of the house, yes," I said.

"Did you go out looking for evidence of some kind?" he asked.

I swallowed hard, my heart skipping. "I suppose I wanted to go and see the area for myself. It's...well, it's hard to believe that he is gone. I don't know why, but I thought seeing the place might...it might give me closure."

It wasn't entirely true, but it wasn't all that far from the truth, either. It was incredibly hard to believe Sam was gone.

"It's just difficult to imagine how someone could have overpowered him," I said.

"You aren't the only one who thinks so..." Sergeant Newton said, and I heard the heaviness in his words. "It's something we have been talking about all day. No one seems to have an answer for how it happened in the first place. It's troubling, that. The men don't like the idea that one of our best officer's was killed so easily. It's terrible. There's no other way to look at it."

"That's too true..." I said.

He sighed on the other end of the line. "Look, Mrs. Lightholder...I don't know about this window having any connection to Sam's death, but I will certainly look into it."

I frowned. "I'm not certain it has any connection either, but it struck me as strange."

"It's not the first time we've had reports of robberies recently, though the reports typically come when those who were away end up returning home," he said. "I'm certain the Mayfields will be pleased to hear that some citizen was kind enough to let us know about the break-in."

I nodded, trying to find a way to get Sergeant Newton to tell me anything else that might be helpful about the case. He was certainly reasonable, but that didn't mean he was going to willingly give me any information that he didn't think I needed.

After all, I wasn't with the police, not officially, and I didn't have any reason to be involved with their business.

"And I should warn you..." he said, dropping his voice. "There are some here at the station who would not take kindly to learning that you called, attempting to interfere once again – "

"I am not attempting to interfere," I said.

"Yes, I realize that," the Sergeant said. "But there are some who would believe otherwise. Those who were not all that fond of Sam's work ethic, nor his inflexibility when it came to the rules. I daresay there are a few who are happy he's gone."

Goose pimples formed on my arms. Was he trying to tell me that they believed it might have been one of the officers at the station who caused all this?

"Those same people are the ones who despised Sam for trusting someone outside the force, someone like you," he said, his voice even lower. "Hypocrites, I know, but they didn't like that he could be a favorite for following the rules, yet be able to get away with breaking them at the same time."

"I never thought of it that way," I muttered.

"Neither did he," Sergeant Newton said. "Which isn't

a problem, exactly, but it certainly didn't make him any more friends."

That didn't strike me as something that would have greatly mattered to Sam, in the end.

"If I were you…" the Sergeant said. "I would keep my distance from this whole business…for your own peace of mind. I wouldn't want you getting caught up in any of the tension happening around here in the aftermath of his death."

The same sort of warning that Sam would have given me, though in a much kinder tone. Out of respect for his friendship with Sam, he wanted to try and protect me.

"Thank you, Sergeant," I said, rather solemnly. "I will do my best."

"Well, Mrs. Lightholder, I need to be getting back to my work," he said, his tone a great deal more casual now. "I appreciate you letting us know about the window, and I promise you that we will find out what happened to Sam. It may take some time, but we have our best men on the job."

"I'm certain you do," I said. "And thank you."

"Have a good day, ma'am," he said, and then hung up the other end of the line.

Regretfully, I placed the receiver back in its place.

*Well, back at square one…*I thought to myself.

I certainly did appreciate the Sergeant doing what he could to protect me from the situation in which I found myself. I didn't want to get caught up in the troubles happening within the police department. It seemed there was more going on there than I'd ever learned about from Sam. Perhaps he was simply unaffected by it, or even uninterested in people's petty ways.

Sergeant Newton had warned me, though, to keep my distance. He didn't want me getting involved. I believed him when he said it was for my own sake, and for my safety. But he didn't realize the sorts of things I'd been through since moving to Brookminster, the terrible sides of people I'd already seen.

He didn't know about my tie to the military, or Roger and his spying, or Sidney and his chasing me around the country, just to steal some letters Roger had written to me.

No...there was a great deal that Sergeant Newton didn't know. To him, I was nothing more than a young woman with a compassionate heart, only wanting to learn the truth of what happened to my friend.

He didn't know that I knew what it was like to see someone's life fade away, because of my actions. I wondered if he'd ever watched someone die, or had to escape someone who was trying to kill him?

In his line of work, especially with his position as a Sergeant, he likely had. But I was sure he never would have expected that of me.

I supposed it just went to show that there was a great deal more to people than what we could see when we looked at them.

I realized I could let it all consume me, and despair in the truth of it. Or I could do what I had done before, and solve the mystery surrounding Sam's death.

I decided the latter was the better choice. And to do that, I was likely going to need some help. Someone who would be able to help me connect the pieces, find hints and clues to Sam's life that might have been missed before.

I would have to trust the investigation of the different police officers to Sergeant Newton. It was obvious that he cared about Sam, and that he had truly considered him a friend. I knew that sort of undertaking would be far too much for me to handle alone.

So I had to leave it to him. And I would.

But that didn't mean I was stepping out entirely.

Not when something else could have happened... something that only I would be able to discover.

6

I realized soon after my phone call with Sergeant Newton that there was a way I could still help with the investigation that would keep me entirely out of the way of the police. They wouldn't even know I was looking into the matter.

The idea came as soon as I went to have afternoon tea with Irene, who had been worrying over me for the last two days.

Sitting in her kitchen, she stared at me across the table, a look on her face like a mother watching her child go through their first heartbreak, helpless yet empathetic.

"I'm sorry you had to experience all this all over again," Irene said. "And so soon after your relationship with him had started to...well, started to bloom, really."

I sighed, shaking my head. "To be honest, Irene, as wonderful as Sam was, and as much as I cared about him, I wasn't entirely sure that I had romantic feelings for him. He was a good man, and I know that he would have taken care of me...but there was something in me that just couldn't find peace with being with another man. Not yet."

Once again, I found myself wanting to tell her about Roger, that he was the reason why I couldn't find peace with the idea of being with Sam. Knowing he was alive, yet not knowing exactly where that left our relationship, did not make me feel as if I had any right to pursue anything else with another man.

The only hint I had that Roger still loved me was that crushed lily I'd found in the rock, which was now hidden safely away between the pages of a book in my room. And if he was still alive, did that mean we were still married in the eyes of the law, even if the rest of the world believed him to be dead?

I had no idea what it all meant, but I did know that I wouldn't have been able to pursue anything with Sam until I did know, one way or another.

"I know, dear..." Irene said, absently spinning her spoon inside her teacup, though her sugar must have long since dissolved. "I can't ever imagine being with anyone else besides Nathanial. But even still, it was clear that Sam really cared about you...he had opened himself up to you, and seemed receptive to the idea of something happening between you both."

I tried to swallow, but my throat had gone dry. "It makes me wonder what his last thoughts might have been..." I said. "I imagine he was frightened, but was he upset because of what I'd said? Or hopeful?" I laid my head down in my arms, which were folded on the table. "I hope he was hopeful...even if I had no intention of following through."

"Oh, sweetheart..." Irene said, reaching across the table to squeeze my hand affectionately.

"This is why I need to figure out what happened to him," I said, lifting my head. "I feel responsible, in a way, for what happened, and I – "

"Oh, not this again," Irene said, shaking her head. "My dear, why is it that you always feel responsible for other people? There is nothing you could have done – "

"What if I had gone out for dinner with him that night?" I asked. "Would that have gotten him away from that alley, so he couldn't have been attacked like he was? Would he still be here?"

"Helen, you are going to drive yourself utterly batty," Irene said. "Please, you cannot torment yourself thinking these things. It amazes me how you can ever get any sleep..."

I pulled the teapot toward myself, and refilled my cup. "What I need to do is find out exactly who in his life might have had a grudge against him," I said. "The police won't help me. Sergeant Newton told me quite blatantly that I needed to keep my distance. He also made it seem like there may have been some men on the force who held grudges against Sam, and they needed to be investigated. How can I be sure that it was just among the police? What about enemies in his personal life?"

I lifted the lid of the sugar bowl, and plucked a few cubes out before stirring them into the hot, steaming tea.

"Which got me thinking..." I said, bringing the tea to my lips, inhaling the earthy, fragrant scent. "There is so little I know about Sam's family. I understand they lived here in Brookminster for many generations. His father was a member of the city council, very well known and liked. I heard that his grandfather owned a farm outside of town, one of the biggest in this part of England. And perhaps the most familiar piece of information would be that Sam had a brother, Walter, who had some sort of bizarre romantic relationship with my aunt Vivian that ended rather abruptly."

"Yes, that is all true," Irene said. "And to be perfectly honest, that is about as much as I know, as well."

I sipped the tea, hesitant as the hot liquid burned my upper lip.

"There has to be more to him than that," I said.

"Well, what about his friends?" Irene asked, laying her chin in one hand, the other drumming on the table-top. "Did he ever mention any?"

"There weren't many chances for those sorts of conversations," I said. "I can't remember him ever discussing anyone...apart from those who had died, or you and Nathanial."

"And I certainly would not have considered us more than acquaintances with him," Irene said.

I tapped my own fingers on the table.

"I wonder what his relationship was like with his family," I said. "I know he was protective of his brother, but what of his parents? Are they still in town?"

"Oh, yes," Irene said. "His father is retired now, but they live just on the outskirts of the village, where they purchased a small farming property. As far as I know, they had a good relationship, but Sam's work always kept him busy. Sometimes I stop and talk with Mrs. Graves at church on Sunday, and she always seems quite chipper."

I scratched the side of my cheek. "Was there ever another Mrs. Graves?" I asked. "Surely I can't have been the first woman that Sam ever found remotely interesting."

Irene's brow furrowed, her grey eyes glued to her teacup. "Oh, dear, I'm not entirely sure..." she said. "Before you came to Brookminster, I cannot be sure I would have paid much attention to his personal life very much. He could have very well been married at one point, but I never would have known."

The door to the teashop opened, and Nathanial stepped through with Michael trailing along behind.

"Hello, dear," Irene said, looking over at the two and smiling. "How was closing up?"

"Fine," Nathanial said. "Though Mrs. Georgianna wished to stay and chat, of course. Apparently her daughter recently gave birth to her third grandchild."

Irene smiled. "Oh, yes, I've heard all about this new bundle of joy," she said. "And you, Michael? Did you help your father?"

"Yes," Michael said, smiling, walking over to us to give his mother a hug. "I helped him bring all the tablecloths into the laundry."

"Wonderful job, my boy," she said, kissing his cheek. She looked over Michael's head to Nathanial, who had also walked over to the table. "Tea, dear?"

"Yes, that'd be lovely," he said.

"Oh, sweetheart, perhaps you can answer this question for us," she said. "Do you know if Inspector Graves was ever married?"

Nathanial looked back and forth between the two of us. "Investigating again, are we?"

I smiled sheepishly up at him.

"No, he was never married," Nathanial said. "It said as

much in his obituary."

"Did that come out today?" I asked. "I didn't even get the paper."

Nathanial nodded. "Let me get it for you."

He retrieved it from the kitchen counter and set it down on the table between us.

"Come along, Michael, we should get you changed for supper," Nathanial said, laying a hand on his son's shoulder. "Let's leave Mummy and Mrs. Lightholder to their tea."

Michael began happily chatting about a book he'd read that day in school, while Nathanial nodded and agreed at the appropriate times.

Irene picked up the paper and flipped through until she located the obituaries. I watched her eyes scan the page. "Ah, here," she said, setting it down before me on the table.

It was rather short, and to my surprise, explained nothing about Sam's life apart from his career. It was as if that was his entire life, and all anyone knew him for.

Frustrated, I looked away. "There has got to be more to him than his job as Inspector," I said.

"Well, short of going to explore his home, I doubt we are going to be able to find out much more," Irene said.

I glanced over at her.

"Don't get any ideas," she warned.

"I don't even know where he lived..." I said. "That's the sort of thing a friend should know, isn't it?"

Irene sighed. "I'm sorry. I suppose so, yes."

Nathanial returned a moment later. "Michael seems determined to read another chapter of this book before we have dinner," he said, taking a seat beside his wife at the table. "You know, as I was back in his room, I realized that Sam never had a wife, but I do think he had a sweetheart some years back."

Irene's eyes widened. "Oh, how could I have forgotten? Yes, there was someone. Oh, what was her name..." She snapped her fingers, her face screwing up with concentration. "Oh! Her name was Valerie Price, wasn't it?"

Nathanial nodded. "I believe so, yes."

"Oh, good heavens, I can't believe I forgot about her..." she said. "I suppose it wasn't so much her that I had forgotten as it was Sam in that situation."

"In what situation?" I asked.

Irene glanced down the hall to ensure that Michael would not be able to overhear. "About, what, three years ago, Nathanial? Yes, during the summer festival, right in the middle of the village, in front of everyone, Sam and this Valerie Price got into a heated argument. At least, I remember her side being quite heated. She was furious about something, though I can't remember what."

"She accused him of secretly seeing someone else, didn't she?" Nathanial asked.

"Oh, that's right," Irene said. "Well, somehow this had all come out during the festival, and she chose then to ask him about it. Her accusations seemed flimsy, but Sam was left standing there in the middle of the street, entirely helpless, as she yelled at him in front of everyone."

"Yes," Nathanial said. "It was uncomfortable for everyone. I remember someone attempting to soothe her, trying to talk to her, but she just shoved them off and continued on her rampage."

"So had he been unfaithful to her?" I asked, now a great deal more curious.

"I have no idea," Irene said. "It seemed to us that he was trying to assure her that he had never done anything like that, but she seemed determined to believe otherwise."

My heart skipped. "Do you think it was possible that she still harbors feelings for him?" I asked. "Or anger toward him for humiliating her?"

"Humiliating her?" Irene asked. "Oh, come now, dear, I think you missed the point of the story – "

"Well, from her perspective, she was humiliated," I said. "Especially if she really believed what she said was true."

"I have a hard time believing she was doing it for more than the attention," Nathanial said. "She was always that sort of woman, who enjoyed causing a scene far too much."

"Though, I suppose it is possible she still had feelings for Sam…" Irene said. "Even though I have not seen them anywhere near one another since."

"And I never heard Sam mention her," I said.

"I don't imagine he would," Nathanial said.

"Well, her reaction might have been enough to question her in his murder," Irene said. "I suppose my only counter to it is that it was three years ago now…"

"Some people harbor grudges for a long time," I said. "Something Sam told me once."

Irene nodded.

"Well, I suppose there is only one way to find out," I said, rising from my seat.

"Where are you going?" Irene asked, her eyebrows

coming together.

"To call this Valerie Price," I said. "May I borrow your telephone?"

Nathanial and Irene exchanged uncertain glances. "I suppose," Irene said.

"And your phone book?" I asked.

"I'll get it," Nathanial said.

After flipping through the pages, we found a one Henry Price, and Nathanial was almost certain it was Valerie's father. Valerie herself was not listed in the book.

"Are you certain you want to do this?" Irene asked.

"Of course," I said. "If it will help us find Sam's killer, than I have to."

Nathanial seemed nervous, and Irene's gaze softened. "Very well," she said. "Go on, then."

I dialed the number and waited.

Irene leaned in to the receiver, clearly hoping to overhear whoever it was that answered.

"Hello?" It was certainly a man's voice on the other end.

"Yes, hello," I said. "Is this Henry Price?" I asked.

"It is," the man said. "Who might be asking?"

"My name is Penelope Driscoll, and I was wondering if Valerie Price was available to speak with?" I asked.

"Valerie?" Henry asked. "Why do you need to speak with her?"

"I'm with the police, Mr. Price, and we are investigating Inspector Graves' death," I said. "I was wondering if she might be around to answer some questions."

"Again?" Henry asked, annoyance tinging his words. "As I told the police before, she is not here. Hasn't been for some time."

"What do you mean?" I asked. "Where is she?"

"In Wales, as I told the Sergeant," Henry said. "She and her husband moved there almost two years ago. She hasn't been back to Brookminster since Christmas."

"I see," I said. *Well, Sergeant Newton was right...they certainly do seem to have this under control, having beaten me to this lead already.* "Do you know if she had any contact with the Inspector before his death?"

"No," Henry said. "Though she did call me yesterday to send her regards to his family after hearing about his death."

I nodded, looking at Irene, who looked rather displeased.

"Well, thank you very much for your time, Mr. Price," I said. "I apologize for disturbing you again."

"Yes, well, see that the information I've given is passed along to those who need it so this doesn't happen again," he said, and then hung up the phone.

I looked at the receiver. "He could have at least said goodbye," I said, setting it back on the hook.

"Well, that lead dried up quickly..." Irene said. "I had no idea she'd been married."

Nathanial said, "If she's been in Wales for the last two years, and married, then I think it's safe to say we can take her off the suspect list, right?"

"I believe so, yes," I said, frowning. "Well, that's discouraging. Not that she wasn't the killer, mind you," I added quickly. "I suppose we are back to where we were before, aren't we?"

"Indeed," Irene said.

"There is no one left in his life to investigate?" Nathanial asked. "Surely there must be someone..."

I pursed my lips together, thinking. "Well, I suppose there is always his parents," I said. "Though that would be difficult to investigate."

"What about his brother?" Irene asked.

I looked over at her. "Walter?" I asked.

Surprised I hadn't considered Walter before, I chewed the inside of my lip. He certainly seemed the type, didn't he? And it wouldn't be the first time that I suspected him of murder...

"A drunkard, isn't he?" Nathanial asked.

"Yes," I said. "And has quite the temper, too, if I remember correctly. Even Sam admitted it."

"But didn't Sam love his brother?" Irene asked. "That doesn't seem like the type of relationship to turn sour."

"Unless Sam attempted to stop him during one of his rages," I said. "And Walter didn't even realize what or who he was attacking..."

"That's a troubling possibility," Nathanial said.

"So what are you going to do?" Irene asked me.

"I don't know..." I said. "Though I must admit, I am not all that keen on investigating a man who has a reputation in town for having a temper and being a drunkard..."

"Then you shouldn't investigate alone," Nathanial said. "Especially if he was the one to kill Sam. He could easily do the same to you, couldn't he?"

"I thought he had done that to my aunt," I said. "I'm afraid I might be a little biased going into this whole thing."

"Then you should tread carefully," Irene said. "Lest you find yourself in a situation that you'll end up regretting."

7

It became quite clear to me soon after that the best way to speak to Sam's brother Walter would be in a public place. And unfortunately for me, the place where that was going to be the most likely was at Sam's funeral a few days later.

It was much harder for me to wake up the morning of the funeral than I thought it might be. I had known for four whole days that Sam was gone. I had walked the alley where he had been killed. Everyone in town knew about it, and was talking about it.

It was much different, however, to be standing in my room, staring at my reflection in the mirror, wearing the same black dress I'd worn to Roger's funeral.

*I have seen this reflection of myself far too often...*I realized. *How many times does this make? How many funerals have I attended? How many will I have to attend in the future?*

I hoped this was the last, as I spun around and looked at myself from all angles in the mirror.

When was the last time I went to a wedding? Or a birthday celebration? Or witnessed the excitement from new parents at the birth of a child? Those are life's joyful moments. Why have I not been able to experience more of them?

I frowned, grabbing my sweater to combat the cooler day, and made my way downstairs.

Irene seemed to understand as I lamented my own self pity on my way to the funeral with her, Nathanial, and Michael.

"It's a season, dear," she said. "We all experience them. Seasons of happiness, and seasons of hardship. I imagine there are many like us who feel as if there is nothing but sad or difficult things happening during this time, especially given the war happening around us. Every day people are receiving heartbreaking news. I'm certain there are good things happening still, but for now, they are quieter, and overshadowed by the more difficult moments in our lives."

"I suppose you're right," I said as we walked. "I'm ready for a change, though."

"We all are, dear," Irene said, taking Nathanial's hand in her own.

In that moment, I wished for Roger's hand to hold the same way.

We weren't the only ones making our way to the church for the funeral. Strolling along the street were most of the townsfolk; I saw Mr. and Mrs. Henrietta, walking arm in arm, Mrs. Henrietta wearing a black hat with a fishnet veil hiding part of her face, white roses pinned to the pill cap. I noticed Mrs. Georgianna, a handkerchief clasped tightly in her hand as she dabbed gently at the side of her face, walking toward the church beside Mr. and Mrs. Trent. Mr. Trent's face was somber, and he stared ahead, his eyes fixed on the steeple.

I saw the Diggory's, as well as the Hodgin's, and I even noticed their children tagging along.

I saw people I hadn't seen in weeks, all making their way toward the church.

*Oh, Sam...*I thought. *All of these people...they're coming to pay their respects to you. I hope you knew how much you were admired while you were here. This just proves it.*

We entered the church after the Diggory's, who acknowledged us with quick, quiet greetings.

The chandeliers overhead glowed brightly, and the pews were polished and filling quickly. Voices spoke in hushed tones, and the organ at the front of the room echoed across the sanctuary as it played its mournful tune.

I frowned as my eyes drifted up toward the altar. Mr. James, who would have been the one giving the funeral service, was now gone as well, having died in August, killed by a man seeking to keep his secrets.

"Oh, isn't that Mr. James' son?" Irene asked in a whisper, pointing up toward the front of the sanctuary.

Nathanial and I followed her pointing finger.

A young man stood off to the side of the pulpit, wearing long, black robes with a white sash around his neck. He spoke in low voices to an elderly man, nodding his head, a look of concern on his handsome face.

"He certainly looks like Mr. James," I said.

"That's his son, all right," Nathanial said. "I heard he might be leaving seminary to take over his father's place. It seems that he has done just that."

I looked up at the young man, who did look so much like his father. "He's so young, though..."

"Indeed," said Nathanial. "But he's a good lad. Has a good head on his shoulders."

"Always has," Irene said. "I think he will do just fine here."

We made our way down the center aisle. I noticed more familiar faces as we went, some of whom turned and smiled at me.

We took our seats in the fourth pew from the front, settling in beside the Diggory's.

"It's such a shame, isn't it?" Mr. Diggory said as we sat. "Whoever would have thought that Sam Graves could have been killed? And so young?"

"I know," Nathanial said to him, adjusting his tie. "It's certainly not something I ever could have anticipated."

"And the fact they haven't figured out who killed him yet?" Mr. Diggory said, his eyes widening.

"Not now, dear," Mrs. Diggory said sternly, laying her hand on her husband's knee. "Not in front of the children.

Both of their sons were peering around their mother, waiting to hear what their father said next.

"To our knowledge they haven't found whoever it was," Nathanial said. "But for all we know, they've already quietly apprehended the criminal and we are all well on our way to safer days once again."

"I certainly hope you're right," Mrs. Diggory said. "I can't stand the thought that another criminal is running around on these streets..."

Just then, Mr. James' son stepped up to the pulpit, clearing his throat as he did. The organist finished the line she was playing before sitting back, eyeing him in a respectful manner.

"Good afternoon, ladies and gentlemen," he said. His voice, clear and strong, echoed across the sanctuary, silencing the last few people who were still speaking. "Thank you for gathering today, as we are here to celebrate the life and service of Samuel William Graves."

William...that's a strong middle name. Yet another thing about Sam I didn't know.

"My name is Timothy James. As some of you know, I have taken my father's place here at the church, but I must admit that this is the first funeral I have ever been responsible for. It breaks my heart that Samuel Graves is the man who I have to honor in this way first, yet at the same time, there are few men that are as respected as he was."

A sniffle sounded somewhere near the front pew, and my eyes fell upon an older woman with grey in her dark hair. The man beside her, the older man that had been previously speaking with the vicar, wrapped his arm around her shoulder, holding her tightly against his side.

I leaned over to Irene and whispered to her, "Is that Sam's mother?" I asked.

Irene nodded to me, her eyes creased with sadness as she watched the poor, older woman cry into a handkerchief.

Young Mr. James continued, "This is truly a sad day for Brookminster, though the Word tells us not to despair when someone passes on from this world. Samuel Graves was a man of faith, who demonstrated the depth of his belief on more than one occasion. My father once said that Sam was like a stream as deep as it was wide, and that nothing could disturb him."

I dipped my head, my own eyes beginning to sting.

*Steady he most certainly was...*I thought to myself, my hands knit together in my lap. *Nothing did shake him, did it?*

More sniffles were heard around the room. As I turned to look, I noticed Mrs. Georgianna dabbing at her eyes once again. Mrs. Trent was blowing her nose into her handkerchief. Mr. Hodgins looked rather stoic, but his bottom lip was stiff and his jaw clenched.

*Sam...you truly left a mark on the hearts of those here in the community...*I thought. *These people here are people you impacted, people you helped. They may never have thanked you the way they should have, but they were appreciative. I hope you knew that.*

It saddened me to think that some of these people had never showed Sam how grateful they were for his service to the community, for his desire to help keep everyone safe. I could see it in their faces now, as clear as day, but had Sam known?

The tears sprang to my eyes, and I couldn't contain them any longer.

I cried, missing the next few minutes of the vicar's message, as he read from different verses about having hope in our eternity, and understanding that our lives were meant for something far greater than ourselves.

I felt a nudge in my arm, and looked up to see Irene looking pointedly at a man a few rows ahead of us.

He looked remarkably like Sam, but perhaps a head shorter. The same dark hair, the same broad shoulders. I could not see his face, but I knew that as soon as he turned around, I would certainly recognize him as Sam's brother, Walter.

He wasn't moving, his shoulders entirely still as he stared up at the vicar. It was almost as if he were made of stone.

Sitting there, dressed in a smart suit, he certainly didn't strike me as the town drunkard that everyone said he was. Looks could be deceiving, though. Sam had taught me that.

I remembered Sam saying his brother might very well have been a lout, but that didn't mean he was a murderer.

Was it possible he was the one to take your life, Sam? I wondered. *If he was...then he is doing an awfully good job at playing the part of the grieving brother, showing up to the funeral.*

But wouldn't that be ideal for the murderer to do? To show up to the funeral?

I glanced over my shoulder at all of the people in the room. My eyes fell on many; the owner of the book store that had been in love with one of the more recent victims, Mr. Hodgin's new assistant at the butcher shop, and even the cook from the inn, who always seemed to have a smile on his face. Not today, though.

Everyone in town was here.

That had to mean that someone here had killed Sam. Perhaps it would have looked strange if someone *hadn't* come, and would have certainly made people question their motives.

Was it you, Walter? Were my initial fears about you not entirely unfounded?

I had no idea...but I had to get to the bottom of it.

For Sam's sake.

8

The service ended a short time later, and the guests were led outside to the churchyard where Sam was to be buried.

I watched with a knot in my chest as the pallbearers walked the casket out into the cemetery. It was hard to believe that Sam was lying in that coffin, soon to be buried beneath the earth, never to be seen this side of heaven again.

Death seemed so final. So fast. I felt as if I had hardly gotten to know him, and he was taken from us.

His parents must have felt it far more acutely than I ever could have. As would any other members of his family. Their loss must have been closer to when I lost Roger.

I noticed Mrs. Graves huddled near her husband, watching the casket move through the cemetery, her eyes red and puffy, her face blotchy. She clutched a handkerchief to her chest, her lips pinched together as she cried without a sound.

Mr. Graves didn't look much better. His face, pale and drained of all color, was flat and expressionless...much like his son's would have been during something like this. It was unsettling seeing just how much Sam's father looked like him...or vice versa, perhaps.

I passed by an ash tree as we moved further through the churchyard...and my heart skipped a beat.

I remembered Sam standing there, watching me as I attended the funeral for the Polish beggar, where I had been the only one to show up. The stern look on Sam's face would be hard to forget, and the disdain radiating from him in the dim afternoon light had sent chills down my spine. He had warned me not to get involved in the investigation of the man's death. He had intimidated me, then, but it wasn't long after that he started to reluctantly trust me.

It was hard to believe he could so recently have been standing there in front of that tree. And now...he was gone.

As we walked, no sound from any of the guests apart from their shuffling footsteps, I looked around.

My eyes fell on the gate where Sam had retrieved me after Mr. James's death. The night that my reputation was very nearly ruined. The night I thought I'd lost Sam's trust, perhaps forever. I could remember his face clearly. The way he'd stared at me from just inside the gate, like I was suddenly a stranger to him. Even still, he'd known I hadn't been the one to commit the murder, but I'd gotten myself mixed up in everything once again. The vicar's blood had been on my hands, streaked across my clothing in my attempts to save him.

My thoughts returned to the present.

There was barely any room to walk as we made our way toward the open grave, which waited eagerly to be filled so that the earth could return to its eternal slumber.

I didn't mind standing back with the Driscoll's, away from the service taking place directly beside the grave. That was definitely meant for his family, and those closest to him. Even though we had been friends, and he had expressed interest, I still didn't feel right standing anywhere near those who had known him for far longer.

I couldn't see the grave from where I stood, nor Sam's casket. It was still hard to wrap my mind around the fact that he was, in fact, lying inside. It just didn't seem possible. Perhaps I was nothing more than a coward, standing back as far as I was, not wanting to lay eyes on what I already knew to be happening up beside the grave.

When Roger had died, as his wife, I'd been forced to stand directly beside the gaping maw that was the hole meant for his body. All I'd wanted to do, however, was to be as far away as I possibly could be. I wanted to run, to flee, from the reality that was my life.

Here, I had the safety and comfort of distance. Protecting myself from yet another ache and another memory that could haunt my dreams. Sometimes, it was better to be selfish in order to ensure that I could hold onto my sanity.

I was glad that Irene didn't urge me forward. Instead, she kept looking over at me, a sad, motherly sort of smile on her face, tears glistening in her eyes. She helped remind me that I was not alone in this moment. Happy for her and Nathanial's company, I waited until we heard the vicar's last few words, difficult to hear as far back as we were, fade into the distance.

"May we all remember to live as Samuel Graves did; with honor, with zeal, and most importantly, with a desire to serve others."

There was a meal to be served in the basement dining hall of the church, where everyone could greet Sam's family and express their condolences. Food, however, was the last thing on my mind, as my stomach had twisted itself into such tight knots, I wasn't even sure I would be able to fit anything inside.

"Perhaps we should go..." I said to Irene, glancing toward the road.

"I don't think we should yet," Irene said. "You should meet his parents. And I thought that you wanted to meet Walter to speak with him?"

"Yes, I do, but..." I said. "This all seemed a great deal easier when I wasn't actually here, at the funeral. Now seeing it at all, I..."

Irene gave me an understanding, sad sort of smile. "Well...this may be the best place to meet him though, right? Didn't you want to meet him in a more public place, in case he...well, he became angry?"

I looked around, finding Walter after a few moments of searching. My heart ached as I realized it was almost as easy as looking for Sam in a crowd...especially given their similarities. "He certainly doesn't seem to be that way today..." I said.

Even still, she was right. If this was a difficult moment for him, having to attend a funeral for his own brother, as it likely was, then how could I be sure he hadn't drunk himself silly before attending the funeral as a way to cope? And if that was what he was known for, would he even care? Why would he bother to care about what others thought of him when he was miserable and hurting?

Irene was right, though. I had to set my emotions aside, as I would certainly despise myself if I were to leave without having gotten the information I'd been looking for.

"All right," I said. "I suppose I could at least meet him here."

"Good," Irene said. "Let's go."

We made our way down to the church's dining hall, which was a spacious room filled with tables, that smelled of freshly baked pies and spiced apple cider. Tables adorned with simple glass vases full of mums were already filled with guests, and a long line of people stretched from the counter where all the food was waiting, all the way to the doorway leading back up to the sanctuary, where Mr. and Mrs. Graves stood.

Walter, however, was nowhere to be found. He certainly wasn't standing beside his parents.

"Let's get in line before we get anything to eat," Nathanial said.

Swallowing hard, I fell into step beside Irene and Nathanial as we moved to take our spot at the end of the line.

"Poor Mrs. Graves..." Irene said, pulling her shawl back up her shoulders. "She looks absolutely devastated."

"Her husband doesn't look much better," I said, my eyes falling on the two of them.

Mrs. Graves shook the hand of Mrs. Georgianna, who'd somehow made it to the front of the line, despite her sizable girth. I watched as she dabbed at her eyes, nodding her thanks to the boisterous woman.

Mr. Graves seemed just as distressed. His brow furrowed as he spoke to Mr. Trent.

"Where is Walter, though?" I asked, looking around.

"Over there," Nathanial said, pointing over my shoulder.

Walter stood near a round table in the corner, ladling spiced cider into a glass cup. All alone, he looked like a giant hovering above the crystal bowl, the ladle looking like a regular spoon in his grip.

"Perhaps you should go speak to him now," Irene said. "While he's alone."

My heart skipped. Right again, Irene was, but that didn't mean I was all that fond of the coming encounter.

Still, I nodded, and started over toward the round table.

The pungent cider made my mouth water as I approached the table. The heavenly scent of cinnamon, nutmeg, and some candied orange peel reminded me of autumn at my grandmother's farm, where I used to pick apples and help her to preserve them for pies, or heat them and mash them for sauce to be enjoyed with a dash of cinnamon. She always made the best pies, and the cider she would bring out for Christmas was very much the same.

Walter tipped the glass back, downing his cider in one, long gulp.

I picked up the ladle and began to fill a glass for myself, wondering how I should begin the conversation.

Walter smacked his lips, letting out a contented sigh. "This was Sam's favorite drink," he said. "His absolute favorite. Probably too much cinnamon in this, though.

Our mother never could quite make it the same way Sam did."

I looked over at him. "You're Walter...right? Sam's brother?" I asked, setting the ladle back down into the punch bowl.

Walter nodded, eyeing the ladle. "That I am. And you're the one that Sam fancied, aren't you?"

I nearly dropped the cup of punch in my hand.

"Helen, or something, yeah?" Walter asked. He shook his head. "Sam told me about you. Said you were quite a remarkable woman. Sharp as a tack, and a better detective than half the detectives he'd ever known. High praise from my brother, let me tell you."

He fished the ladle out of the bowl once again, filling the small, glass cup in his hand.

I didn't know how to respond to his surprising statement. He seemed so utterly indifferent about it all. Was he at all troubled about the fact that his brother had just passed away?

"So that is you, isn't it?" Walter asked, downing his second cup just as quickly as the first.

"Well...my name is Helen, yes, and your brother and I did know one another—" I said.

"You make it sound like you were nothing more than acquaintances," he said, going for yet a third glass of cider. "Modest on top of everything, are you?"

I wasn't quite sure what I'd expected when I'd considered meeting Walter. The only things I'd known about him were the things I'd learned from others in town, like Sam and Irene. For some reason, he seemed more aloof than I'd expected...but something told me that was nothing more than a cover to shield his true hurt about losing his brother.

"I'm sorry about Sam," I said, my voice cracking as I said it. "He...he was a wonderful man, and losing him was..."

Why couldn't I form the words? Not only that, but the entire reason why I'd come over here to talk to him was to assess whether or not I thought he might have been capable of being the one who killed Sam in the first place. Why was I apologizing to him if he could be, in fact, the murderer?

Walter's face faltered in that moment, his gaze distant as he stared down at the bowl of punch. He pursed his lips, his jaw working, nostrils slightly flared.

I feared an angry outburst. Red spots formed on his cheeks like the apples of the cider he kept drinking.

He looked down suddenly, setting his cup on the table. "I feel as if I should apologize to you..." he said in a low voice, seemingly unable to meet my gaze. "I spent the last few years being a terrible man to my brother, but here you are, at the start of a brand new, promising rela-tionship with him, and he – " He rubbed his chin, taking a steadying breath through his nostrils. "I'm sorry. I cannot imagine how hard this must all be for you right now."

Once again, I didn't know what to say in response.

From his perspective, I could see how he had come to that conclusion. All he knew about me was that his brother had feelings for me, and had started to pursue a relationship with me. What he didn't know, though, was that I'd already gone through this before with my husband.

Regardless, it was still difficult. I may have realized I didn't wish to have any sort of romantic relationship with Sam, but that didn't mean I didn't care for him. If Roger had never reappeared in my life, if I'd never learned that he was still alive, then I knew my feelings toward Sam probably would have been much different. And if that had been the case, then it was likely that I would have been much more upset. To have lost two men that I'd been romantically invested in...that would have been unthinkable.

I didn't have the heart to correct Walter, to tell him that I had not been involved with his brother. I realized it was best not to encourage the thought, either. I didn't want to lie to him or mislead him, especially if I wanted him to trust me.

"How are you holding up?" I asked. I couldn't quite explain it, but as I looked at him, I thought I saw the smallest reflection of Sam in his face. It was in his eyes, which seemed to pierce right through the wall that he was staring at. It made my heart ache, and I found my breath catching in my chest.

"Things have certainly been better," Walter said, shaking his head. "I never in my wildest dreams thought Sam would be gone before I was. If anything, I thought he would end up the one finding me in some back alley somewhere, having died from alcohol poisoning or something..."

My throat grew tight, and the bile rising in my chest made it impossible to take even a sip of the cider in my hand.

I set the cup down on the table, staring down at my hands, silence falling between the two of us.

"It's just..." he began. "I don't know what to do. I wake up in the morning, thinking about something that I want to share with him, only to pick up the telephone, and realize he will never answer...it simply doesn't seem real. I can't believe he's gone."

The cracks around my heart deepened. "I understand that feeling all too well, Walter..."

He downed the rest of his cider, and looked over at me. "Yes, well...I suppose it will all get easier, won't it? At least that's what the younger Mr. James keeps telling me. Who would have thought the vicar's son would come back and taken his father's place..."

He set his cup down and turned, making his way to stand beside his parents.

I wandered back over to where Irene and Nathanial were, my heart aching.

"Well?" Irene asked. "What did you learn?"

"Nothing," I said. "At least, nothing in regards to Sam's death. Walter is...well, he is devastated, to say the least... and at the same time, he still had the consideration to apologize to me for what I'd been through in all of this."

"That's very kind of him," Nathanial said, his eyes drifting over toward where Walter stood with his parents.

"I just couldn't bring myself to ask..." I said. "I know he might be my best lead, though. So I suppose I'll just have to find another way to talk to him."

I looked over at him, and noticed him watching me. He gave me a tight, small smile, and nodded at me.

I nodded in return.

I would have to learn more from him. I owed it to Sam...regardless of how sorry I felt for Walter now.

9

As suspected, I regretted not taking the chance to speak to Walter further about Sam and his death while at the funeral. Even though I was fully aware that he likely wouldn't have been in any sort of mood to have discussed it in the first place, I realized it still would have saved me a great deal of trouble.

I spent the next week looking for a chance to speak with him again. It certainly did not help that I had no idea how to contact him, other than to look him up in the phone book and hope he wouldn't be confused by my call.

"It would certainly be much easier if I were to just happen across him," I said as I sat at the small, round table in the corner of Irene's teahouse. She'd forbidden me from working for at least a fortnight after Sam's death, but seemed to have no qualms with me coming over and spending the afternoons with her after I'd closed up the haberdashery. "It wouldn't be chance, of course. I wish I knew more about him."

"I wish I did, too," Irene said, topping off my cup of tea for the third time that hour. "I don't think the man has been able to hold a job for more than a few months at a time, however. Last I knew, he was ferrying food for Mr. Diggory to some of the farms outside of town, but that was nearly six months ago…"

I sipped the tea, the warmth enough to keep the chill of the cold September afternoon at bay. "And you don't suppose he would still be working there, do you?" I asked.

Irene shook her head. "I can't imagine so, no. I suppose you could go and ask Mr. Diggory, see if he knows where Walter happened to go after Mr. Diggory surely fired him."

I frowned. "I don't know if he would want to tell me, especially if they left off on such poor terms."

The bell chimed above the door, and Irene glanced over her shoulder at the new customers streaming in. "I'll be back," she said, and then wound her way through the tables to the couple rubbing their hands together gratefully in the warmth of the teashop.

As the man removed his hat, I realized it was, in fact, Mr. Diggory.

I sat up a little straighter. What luck!

"Good afternoon, Mr. Diggory," Irene said. "Please find a seat wherever you'd like, and I'll be right out with the specials for the day."

"Thank you very much, Irene, but I cannot stay," Mr. Diggory said. "I was just in town on an errand for our cook, but it's so blasted cold out there, I thought my fingers might freeze."

"Well, I'd be happy to make you a quick cup to warm you up," Irene said.

She turned and gave me a rather pointed look.

"In the meantime, I'm certain that Mrs. Lightholder would love to keep you company," she said, smiling.

Mr. Diggory looked up as I rose from my seat.

Thank you, Irene! I thought, picking up my own teacup and making my way toward the door. This was the perfect chance to ask questions without seeming nosy.

"Hello there, Mr. Diggory," I said, meeting him near the door as Irene excused herself to the kitchen for his tea.

"Good afternoon, Mrs. Lightholder," he said, nodding at me. "How are you this unseasonably cold day?"

"I had the very same idea that you did," I said. "Tea was precisely what I needed to warm up."

"Indeed," he said.

"I trust your family is well?" I asked. "How is Mrs. Diggory?"

"Quite well, thank you," he said. "Though this weekend was hard for her. Not only was it our late son's birthday, but it was also Inspector Graves' funeral. What does it say when a funeral was easier to attend than to sit around at home, pondering over the fact that our son was not there to celebrate with us, nor would he ever be?"

"It certainly has been a hard few months for those in Brookminster," I said. "There have been too many deaths."

"Indeed...and too many of them of a malicious nature," he said. "Mr. Graves' death was the proverbial nail in the coffin. I don't know how our little town could take another blow like that."

"Nor do I," I said.

"I think the worst part of it all is that we don't know who killed the Inspector," Mr. Diggory said. "If the police knew, wouldn't they have let us know that it had been handled? Don't they know we are worried that what happened to him could just as easily happen to any of the rest of us?"

"I'm certain the police are doing whatever they can, Mr. Diggory," I said, finding myself parroting everything that Sergeant Newton had ultimately said. "This took them by surprise as much as it did all of us."

Mr. Diggory turned to look out the window, his hands on his hips. "It isn't as if we can blame some faceless enemy..." he said, his voice dropping. "That would be far easier. Instead, I have to look into the faces of all the different people in this town and wonder who could possibly have the Inspector's blood on their hands..."

His thoughts echoed my own, and I wished I could tell him that as frankly as he'd told me. If I was to get the information I needed, I knew I was going to need him to be cooperative. And that might mean steering the conversation slightly.

"I met Sam's brother at the funeral," I said. "He seemed terribly distressed by all this as well, not knowing who it might have been that attacked Sam in that alleyway."

"Walter?" Mr. Diggory asked, looking over his shoulder at me. "To be honest, I was surprised he was able to pull himself together enough to attend. I assumed he would have been in a drunken stupor somewhere, completely unaware of what had happened in the first place..."

"He seemed entirely in his right mind," I said. "Perhaps just for that one day?"

"Perhaps," Mr. Diggory said. "Although, there have been rumors that he has been trying to clean himself up. In fact, I heard from Mr. Hodgins that Walter had been hired to do some patching on some houses on the eastern side of town. Since Sidney Mason is no longer with us, there are a great many odd jobs around the village that have seemingly gone unfinished." Mr. Diggory shook his head, sighing heavily through his nostrils. "That man may not have been here for very long, but he was an invaluable member of our community. Brookminster was beginning to thrive underneath his care, and I would be lying if I said I didn't miss his sunny disposition and willingness to help at any time."

"Yes..." I said. "I miss that as well." While I couldn't admit that I didn't miss Sidney at all, because of his treachery, and also couldn't admit that he had been a German spy, I could admit that I missed the man I thought he was. He had been helpful, even if it had all been a lie...

I pushed those thoughts from my mind, and returned my attention to the question at hand.

"So...Walter seems to be trying to better himself?" I asked. "Where did you say he was taking those small jobs?"

"Out in the eastern side of town," Mr. Diggory said. "I believe he is working for a one Mr. Adams."

"Well, good for him," I said. "Perhaps having something to keep his mind occupied will be good for him."

"Perhaps it will be," Mr. Diggory said. "I certainly hope he cleans up his act, as he – "

"Here we are, Mr. Diggory," Irene said, reappearing in the dining room, carrying a thermos of tea meant for outdoor traveling.

"Oh, Mrs. Driscoll, I couldn't possibly take this," he said. "I'd be happy to just drink a cup quickly – "

"Nonsense," Irene said. "Take it. Just make sure to bring it back. It's Nathanial's favorite when he takes Michael out fishing. Besides, I know you're a very busy man. Please, it's no trouble at all," she said as he opened his mouth to protest.

Mr. Diggory left soon after, leaving a sizable payment for Irene that I was certain she would have refused if she'd noticed it lying on the hostess stand.

"It seems that Walter has started taking on odd jobs that our friend Sidney Mason would have done once upon a time," I said to Irene in a low voice after some time had passed.

She looked at me sidelong. "Is he now? Well, that's interesting."

"Interesting indeed," I said. "And I believe I know where I might be headed now."

Irene convinced me not to go that night, saying it was possible that he and the other workers may very well have cleaned up for the day. Agreeing, I decided that first thing after I closed up the haberdashery tomorrow, I was going to go and speak to Walter again.

I HEADED out from my shop at three sharp, having had to usher out Mrs. Georgianna, who seemed to want nothing more than someone to calm her as she wept over the Inspector's death like she had at the funeral.

The cold weather was still hanging around after yesterday. All morning, I'd heard hardly anything apart from the fact that it was so much colder this year than it had been in years past in September. Even with the sun shining overheard, it was still chilly enough that the wind seemed to cut right through the fabric of my jacket.

My cheeks were flushed by the time I made it across town, but I cared little as I heard the sounds of hammers and saws further along the road.

I came upon a group of men outside a rather rundown looking cottage just a short distance down from the house that belonged to Miss Harmon, the woman who'd recently killed a widow out of jealousy, leaving her young daughter and a mystery behind. The roof looked as if it had been struck by a fallen tree, and the lovely yellowed stone walls had cracked along the bottom.

A man stood beside the wall with a bucket of some sort of cement in his hands, slathering it against the wall. Another measured the length of the broken window, biting down on a pencil between his teeth in concentration.

Walter was there, too, up on the roof of the house, hammering some tiles into the roof while another man beside him ripped broken tiles out.

A rather rotund man with a protective hat on his head turned to look at me. "No one who isn't a worker is allowed on this site," the man said, his brow furrowing.

I stepped up to the fence. "My apologies, sir. I was just hoping to get a word with Walter. Just for a moment, of course. I can see how busy you are."

There were glances from several of the workers, and the man in charge, likely Mr. Adams, sighed as he turned to look up at the rooftop.

"Graves!" the man shouted, cupping his hands over his mouth. "There's a woman here to see you."

Walter stopped his hammering and looked down, his eyes falling on Mr. Adams for a brief moment, and then sliding over to me. His gaze widened, and his mouth hung slightly open in surprise.

He climbed down off the roof and started over toward me.

"Mrs. Lightholder," Walter said, wiping his dirty hands on a cloth he procured from the back pocket of his trousers. "To what do I owe this pleasure?"

I glanced over his shoulder, seeing more than one pair of eyes watching us, almost eagerly, to overhear just the smallest bit of our conversation.

I hadn't considered how this might look, or who might talk when they heard I'd gone to visit Sam's brother.

"Could we talk for a moment?" I asked, realizing that the best thing I could do was get him away from the others.

His brow furrowed for a moment. "Yes, I suppose that's all right," he said.

Mr. Adams watched us cautiously as we walked away, just down the street.

"Is everything all right?" Walter asked. "You look quite worried about something."

The truth was, this was not the most subtle I'd been about finding information, was it?

I had to think quickly, knowing that I needed him to

tell me one way or another if he was the one who had killed his brother. I needed to catch him off guard enough to startle him, but also ensure I did my best not to evoke the anger he was so well known for.

So without any further thinking, I pretended to burst into tears.

Hiding my face behind my hands, I turned away from Walter, laying it on as thick as I possibly could.

"I'm – I'm sorry," I sobbed, still shielding my face from him. "I don't know what's wrong with me. I – I just can't make sense of any of this."

Walter was making nervous sounds behind me, and I heard him shuffling around. "Oh – Mrs. Lightholder, I – What can I do? What's happened?"

I continued to cry, feeling my face grow hot and tears surprisingly springing to my eyes as I willed them there.

"Here, please, Mrs. Lightholder...won't you sit down? Can I get you something? A drink, perhaps?" he asked.

I nodded, and allowed him to guide me back to a park bench alongside the road.

I sat, trying to take calming breaths. Now that I'd started with the tears, I was finding it somewhat difficult to calm my nerves.

"I'll be right back, as soon as I find you a drink – " he said.

I reached out and laid my hand on his arm, shaking my head. "N – no, it's all right," I said. "I am sorry, Walter, I just..." I wiped my eyes with the back of my hand.

He reached into his front pocket and procured a handkerchief.

I took it, somewhat concerned about whether or not it

was clean, and so I held it tightly between my hands in my lap, sniffling.

"Whatever has happened to you, Mrs. Lightholder?" he asked, taking a seat on the bench beside me.

I looked up at him, not doing anything to hide the tear stains on my cheeks. "To be quite honest, Walter, I am just beside myself about your brother. I cannot sleep, I cannot eat...I just cannot stop thinking about whoever it was that could have done this...this *terrible* thing to your brother."

I clutched the handkerchief tightly in my hands.

"I just cannot understand how someone could do such a thing..." I said, and I looked Walter in the eye. His were the same shade of blue as Sam's. "Who, Walter? Who would have done this?"

Walter stared at me, searching my face, sorrow filling his own. "I..." he said.

My heart skipped as I stared at him, willing him to admit it to me, willing him to confess.

"I have no idea..." he said, his voice cracking, and turned away from me.

He rose from the bench, walking a few steps away, rubbing his chin with his fingers.

"It's the same question that's been tormenting me," he said, stopping, hands on his hips, his voice low. "And why wouldn't it be? Sam was...well, he saved my life."

I blinked at him. "Saved your life?" I asked. "What do you mean?"

"Well, maybe not in the way you're thinking," Walter said. "But he was the reason why I've stopped drinking. I hated it, hated him for it. He pushed me, over and over. It was tough, and I was furious with him most of the time...

but then things started to get easier. I started to feel more...well, like myself."

He sighed, looking down at the ground.

"I'm indebted to him, for the miracle that he brought into my life. He never gave up on me, and then..." he shook his head. "He was gone. Just like that. One call on the telephone, and I learned my brother, my rescuer, was gone."

My heart sank as I stared at him. This was not the sort of thing a man who'd murdered his own brother would say, was it? Walter truly loved Sam. I could see it as clear as day on his face.

"You know..." Walter said. "I've been doing a great deal of thinking since I've given up alcohol. And...well, I realized how terrible I was to your aunt. I know she's gone, now, too, but I really did care about her. She really was a wonderful woman, and I certainly never deserved her, especially given the way I treated her. I wish I could have been better back then, so things could have maybe worked out between the two of us."

That touched my heart in a way I had not expected. Suddenly, I felt terrible for lying to him the way I had, emotionally manipulating him into telling me what he had about his brother.

"Thank you..." I said to him. "I'm certain she would have appreciated those sentiments. She cared for you. Just like your brother did."

I saw his face fall, and he nodded at the ground.

"Yes," he said. "If only I had the chance to tell them both that now."

10

I was back at square one. Not for the first time, of course, but it was always frustrating when all of the suspects I'd found ended up being innocent.

It wasn't as if I wanted any of the suspects to be guilty. I didn't like the idea of anyone being found to be a murderer...especially to be the killer of a friend like Sam Graves. It was unsettling, though, realizing I was still many steps away from discovering who had been the one to kill him in the first place, and I felt quite downtrodden because of it. Who knew if the murderer would strike again to keep someone quiet? What if they figured out I was attempting to get at the truth?

Regardless, I knew there was nothing more I could do without some more outside information.

As I stood at my window, overlooking the steely grey morning outside, I missed Sam. Really missed him. If he was here, we would have figured this case out long ago.

Almost three weeks had gone by since his death, and

life in Brookminster was starting to go back to normal. His name was mentioned less by the customers coming into my haberdashery. I saw fewer troubled faces out in the street, as if people had somehow forgotten what had happened. I heard more laughter, and parents seemed less frightened to allow their children to play outside after dark.

I shouldn't have been surprised, but for some reason, I found myself becoming angry with these people. How could they be so insensitive? Weren't they afraid? Losing such a prominent member of the community...that wasn't just a minor inconvenience. This meant something darker was afoot, didn't it?

I pulled my cup of tea closer to myself, allowing the steam to caress the side of my face.

I cannot make them feel sorrow for Sam, I realized. *Yet I wish people would not so easily return to normalcy. It makes his life feel cheap and wasted.*

I knew that wasn't true, given the sheer number of folk who had showed up for his funeral, and those that had grieved for weeks.

Eventually, life had to return to normal. There was no choice. And in the grand scheme of things, it was certainly better than wallowing in sorrow for so long.

I needed more information if I was going to wrap this case up any time soon. The only place I was going to find that information was from the police station.

Sergeant Newton was my best bet. He'd warned me to keep my distance, the same way that Sam had so many months ago...but like I did then, I had to ignore orders.

I readied myself that morning, adorning a comfortable, conservative outfit in dark blue. Black may have been asking for too much attention, showing I still grieved for Sam, even when I didn't feel as if I'd earned the right to do so. Blue was safer, but would certainly still demonstrate my desire to respect Sam and his death. I also hoped it would help me to go unnoticed by that witch who worked at the reception desk.

I headed out before too long, leaving a note on my door assuring my customers that I would be open that day, but would be opening later than usual. It was Thursday, so I knew this would likely upset Mrs. Haymitch, but I was more prepared for her anger than for Mrs. Georgianna's, who had the ability to make me feel guilty with nothing more than a simple phrase.

The police station seemed quiet that morning, something I was incredibly grateful for. No line out the door, nor were there many people waiting just inside. No more than two men ahead of me, likely with nothing all that complicated or life threatening.

I waited toward the back, as patiently as I could, doing my best to avoid eye contact with anyone up at the front. My heart was beating erratically, my throat tight, and my mouth dry. I didn't want to see them, but I had to do this for Sam.

The two men in front of me cleared the line quickly; one was delivering a package, and the other looking to pay a parking fine he'd received.

Rachel the receptionist directed him away from her desk toward a sign posted on the hallway. "Don't take any other turns, sir, or you might find yourself lost."

She might have been pretty, if it wasn't for the fake

smiles she pasted on her face whenever she looked up at the people entering the station.

She turned her gaze up to me as I approached the desk, and her eyes nearly snapped shut, becoming nothing more than thin slivers, like a snake's.

"Well, well, if it isn't the little deceiving spy?" Rachel sneered, wrinkling her nose at me. "What could you possibly want here? Sam's dead."

I glared at her. "You could be a bit more respectful of the dead," I said.

Rachel met my glare with her own. "Oh? And what about you? Coming to see if he left you in his will or something?"

I gaped at her. This woman had a great deal of nerve, didn't she? I bit my tongue, though, the retort hanging there nasty and clever, and decided against it. I didn't need her to throw me out before I got what I'd come for. "I need to speak to Sergeant Newton," I said in as flat of a voice as I could.

"Sergeant Newton?" Rachel repeated back to me. "What could you possibly want with him?"

"That's not your concern," I said. "It's rather important, though, so if you could please direct me to where his office is – "

"I think not," Rachel said with a harsh chuckle. "He didn't say anything to me about visitors today. Especially not you."

"He isn't expecting me," I said. "But I would still like to – "

"Just who do you think you are?" Rachel hissed. "You come in here, time after time, expecting these men to just drop whatever it is they are doing to – "

"Rachel, is everything all right?"

A chill ran down my spine as I looked up to see Officer Locklier, who had once worked with Sam. I had seen him around before and he'd never had any liking for me.

He looked as menacing as I remembered. The same perfectly trimmed dark hair, the same narrow jaw, the same beady grey eyes.

"Ah, Mrs. Lightholder…" he said in a cool tone. "What a surprise to see you here. Hadn't you heard? Sam Graves is dead. I'm terribly sorry to be the one to tell you, but he won't be here any longer for you to bother."

"I am well aware of Sam's passing," I said. "I was devastated when I heard – "

Locklier rolled his eyes. "Devastated, were you? How long did you know him? Nothing more than a few months? Not nearly long enough for him to make a true impact on you."

I could only stare at him. How dare he speak to me like that!

"What do you want?" he asked. "Trying to sink your claws into someone new, are you?"

"I'm here to see Sergeant Newton," I said. "And I would really appreciate it if – "

"No, sorry," Locklier said, grabbing a stack of files in a folder hanging on the wall beside the reception desk. "You can't."

"Why?" I asked.

"Because there is nothing you need to say to him that you can't say to us, or leave in a request," he said. "We are very busy around here, and we don't have time to deal with your petty problems."

Petty problems? If he knew I was here investigating Sam's death, would he think that was petty as well?

"I'll ask you, then, what you were here to see him about," Locklier said. "Unless you're too embarrassed to say."

"I'm not embarrassed," I said. "But it has nothing to do with you. Is there no such thing as privacy?"

"Not in this place, no," Locklier said. He glanced through the first few pages of the files he'd grabbed from the wall beside the desk. "Now, if you don't care to share the reason for your visit, I'll kindly ask you to turn around and leave the station. We have far more important matters to deal with today, and you are doing nothing more than wasting our time."

Fuming, I realized he would not allow me to see the Sergeant. Entirely at his mercy, and not wanting to cause a scene, I decided the best course of action was to just comply.

"Fine," I said, turning on my heel. I made my way from the station, hearing the subtle sounds of Rachel and Locklier whispering behind me.

I stepped out into the cool late September morning, my blood boiling in my veins.

I had never been treated so horribly in all my life. To have someone be so utterly unkind, so inconsiderate...

No chance to speak with Sergeant Newton. It looked as if that opportunity might not ever come, unless I managed to lie to Rachel over the phone or something, and I couldn't imagine that Sergeant Newton would be exactly pleased to find out I'd lied to get in touch with him –

"Helen, wait!"

I turned, and to my surprise, Constable Chamberlin hurried out the door after me, a look of worry on his face.

I hadn't seen him since the day Irene had brought him to my house, when we were investigating the death of my aunt Vivian. He had been there the night they'd found her body, and had willingly come forward to tell me the strange circumstances surrounding her death.

"Constable Chamberlin," I said, my eyes widening. "What are you – "

"Come with me," he said in a low voice, glancing over his shoulder. "And keep our conversation ordinary."

I listened to him, and we began walking down the street.

"Well...how are you doing?" he asked. "How is life treating you?"

"Things are quite good, thank you," I said. "And how have you been? How is your family?"

"Doing very well, thank you," he said. I could see that his focus was on everyone around us, and not our conversation. His eyes darted over every face, and he continually looked over his shoulder.

He took a right down the next side street, which was more residential than High Street. A lovely park was tucked away between the library and a home that I believed belonged to the Mayfield's. He turned into the park, which seemed entirely empty apart from the trees slowly losing their autumn leaves, as well as the gurgling stone fountain in the center of the path.

"All right, it should be safe to talk here," he said, dropping his voice as he ducked behind a rather scraggly looking bush. "I'm sorry to usher you away like that, but I didn't want anyone to overhear us."

"What happened?" I asked. "How did you – "

"I saw you speaking to Locklier," Chamberlin said, his nose wrinkling. "The man has been insufferable since Sam passed away."

"I can imagine that..."

Chamberlin gave me a pointed look. "Did I overhear you correctly? You were hoping to speak to Sergeant Newton?" he asked.

"Yes," I said. "It was about something rather important."

"Does it have to do with Sam's murder?" Chamberlin asked.

Some of the color drained from my face. "How...how did you know?"

He licked his lips, looking around, even though we were very much alone. "Sergeant Newton is the one who has been in charge of investigating Sam's murder," he said. "He was Sam's closest friend in the station, and I know for certain he was one of the few people that Sam trusted."

"Why are you telling me this?" I asked.

"Because I know you truly care about the outcome of all this," Chamberlin said. "I don't care if there was anything happening between you and the Inspector or not. I do not involve myself in spreading rumors. But all the speculations surrounding Sam's death..."

"What sort of speculations?" I asked.

Chamberlin glanced over the bush before he leaned in closer to me. "I overheard Sergeant Newton speaking with the chief yesterday. It seems the autopsy report for Sam finally came back."

"What took it so long?" I asked.

"I'm not sure," Chamberlin said. "Perhaps since the victim was a member of the police force, they spent a great deal of time working on the report."

"Even after the body had already been buried?" I asked.

Chamberlin nodded, his brow furrowed. "It could have been because of what they found when they did the autopsy. It...well, it was troubling to say the least."

My heart skipped a beat. "How so?"

"He was...are you certain you wish for me to tell you this?" he asked.

"Yes," I said without even considering. "I've been trying to do what I could to help figure this all out as well."

"Well...it seems that he was killed in an unconventional way," Chamberlin said. "His body was punctured in multiple places, but it wasn't with a weapon, exactly. It was a piece of glass, part of which broke off and into his flesh."

A shiver ran down my spine, and I stared up at him. "A piece of glass?" I asked. A thousand questions ran through my mind, and I wondered what in the world had happened to cause that sort of murder. "Was it a crime of passion? Or maybe spur of the moment?"

"That was the chief's thought," Chamberlin said. "But Sergeant Newton seems to be of the opinion that this might have been the work of someone who didn't want the evidence being drawn back to themselves. He thinks it was someone who had experience with killings."

The bile rose in the back of my throat. "Who are they suspecting it might be?" I asked.

"They don't know," Chamberlin said, running his

hands over his face, his gaze distant. "But I, like them, have worried that it might actually be someone...close to home."

"You mean on the police force?" I asked, startled. "But why would another officer kill him? It doesn't make any sense."

"You only saw Sam's perception of the station," he said. "There were many who were jealous of him and his position. Sam could get away with anything he wanted, but he never took advantage of that. He did everything by the book, and if anyone else stepped out of line, he made sure to let them know."

"I understand that made many others angry," I said. "Especially those who enjoyed skirting their responsibilities or coasting through their jobs."

"Exactly," Chamberlin said. "The chief wonders if it might have been someone vying for Sam's job. He always received the interesting cases, and was paid quite well. There are many during these war-torn times who would give almost anything to make sure they can provide better for their families...or for themselves."

"You think someone on the force might have taken things that far? Out of jealousy?" I asked. It wasn't as if I hadn't heard of people killing for less, but even still...

"It's possible," Chamberlin said. "However...*my* fear is that it could have been someone in the military. Between that camp outside of town, the injured soldier's hospital at the manor, and all of the rumors pegging Sidney Mason as a German spy, it wouldn't surprise me if there was a great deal more going on beneath the surface that we never knew about."

It was as if I'd swallowed a stone.

"I just wonder if Sam was getting close to something that he was never supposed to," he said.

This couldn't be happening. I'd been so careful, so incredibly careful –

"Helen, are you all right?" he asked. "I'm terribly sorry, I shouldn't have put all this on you. I – "

I wasn't listening. Had I somehow inadvertently brought this upon Sam? Had his involvement in my life somehow been the reason he'd been killed.

"Chamberlin, I'm fine," I said, trying to force a smile. "But if it's all right with you, I should like to go on home now. I'm worried that if you are away from the station too long, others will notice."

His eyes widened. "You're right. As I said, I am sorry about telling you all this. It's possible that none of it is true. But I do know that the Sergeant and the chief are working hard to locate Sam's killer. And then we can all rest easy."

"Yes, I certainly hope so," I said.

I started off toward home soon after, bidding Chamberlin goodbye. My thoughts quickly turned to Sam, though, and the possibility that it had been someone in the military who had taken his life.

I had been very careful to not tell Sam specifics, especially with anything in regards to Roger's death, or in reality, his faked death. I also had not told Sam the details of Sidney's death, which was closely tied to Roger.

How could anyone have known, apart from Sam and me? I knew he wouldn't have told anyone what little he knew, and I certainly hadn't said anything...

That wouldn't matter, though, would it, if they

suspected that he did know everything I knew. That would make him a hazard, a liability.

And a piece of glass would be much harder to trace than a knife or a gun, wouldn't it?

11

I had a difficult time digesting everything that Chamberlin had shared with me. It seemed entirely unreal, thinking it could have been one of the police, or even worse...someone in the army.

More than that, was Sam's connection to me what ended up getting him killed in the end?

It was as if a knife had been lodged in my chest as I made my way back into the heart of town.

I needed to talk to someone. And the only person I could think to speak with was Irene. She may have been one of the few people left that I could trust.

I made straight for the teahouse, my heart beating rapidly in my chest. Worried that I was going to be too early, I lingered outside the front door, looking in.

The door swung inward a moment later, and Nathanial peered outside. "Helen, what are you doing out there?" he asked, rubbing his arms with his hands. "It's terribly cold outdoors. Please, come inside."

I didn't argue, as the temperature certainly seemed to be dropping.

The teahouse was incredibly warm. The fireplace against the eastern wall was full of crackling logs, filling the room with a comfortable glow. There were quite a few customers strewn about the room, enjoying the soothing tea that Irene and Nathanial offered to them, along with freshly baked cakes and breads.

"Is everything all right?" Nathanial asked, taking my coat from me. "I don't mean to sound rude, but you look as if you might be falling ill."

"I'm not entirely sure that I'm not," I said. I looked up at him. "Is your wife around? There's something rather important that I need to discuss with her."

"Certainly," he said. "Though I must warn you, we've been busy today with all this cold weather. You may not have her attention for long."

"That's fine," I said. "I don't think it will take me long to tell her what I need to."

He guided me over to the kitchen. "Are you going to be all right?" he asked.

"Yes, of course," I said. "It's nothing to do with me."

At least...I certainly hoped it wasn't.

I stepped into the kitchen and found Irene with her back to me, wooden spoon in one hand, and a large ceramic bowl in the other, mixing feverishly.

"Darling, Helen is here to see you," Nathanial said. "Would you like me to watch the front of the shop for a few moments while she speaks with you?"

Irene wheeled around, her grey eyes wide. "Helen, hello," she said. "Yes, of course, Nathanial, thank you."

Nathanial nodded and excused himself from the kitchen.

"How are you doing today?" Irene asked, setting the bowl down on the counter and hurrying over to me, wrapping her arms tightly around me in a hug. "It's been nearly a week since I've seen you. I've been worried about you."

When she pulled away, I noticed flecks of flour on her cheeks, and the dough clinging to the sleeves of her dress.

"I'm sorry," I said. "I've been...well, things at the shop have been busy, and I...I don't know. I suppose I haven't been much up for socializing."

Irene's brow furrowed. "Why's that, dear? What's troubling you?"

She picked up the bowl once more and pressed it into my hands. Many hands certainly made for light work. The dough smelled of cinnamon and currants, and my stomach grumbled. Oh, how I wished that all I had to concern myself with was what delicious baked goods Irene made to enjoy.

"Helen?" Irene asked.

I looked up, realizing I'd been pondering over the dough in the bowl for longer than necessary.

"I'm sorry," I said. "I just...well, I heard some troubling news this morning."

She walked over to the stove where she had been glazing a freshly baked batch of scones. "Oh?" she asked, glancing over her shoulder. "How so?"

I settled into a stool before picking up the spoon and beginning to turn the currants over in the bowl. "Well, after speaking with Walter last week, I realized I was back at square one," I said. "So I decided to do the only thing I could think to do, and that was to go see Sergeant Newton down at the police station."

Irene wheeled around, glaze dripping down the spoon in her hand. "The police station? I thought you said you were never setting foot in there again?"

"I thought that was true," I said. "But what other choice did I have?"

Irene pursed her lips, exhaling through her nose. "Well, you could have just sat back and allowed the police to solve this murder. Perhaps they already have."

"They haven't," I said. "In fact, they're far from it, I'm afraid."

"I take it you spoke with the Sergeant?" she asked.

I shook my head. "No. I tried, but was chased from the station by their witch of a receptionist, as well as someone called Officer Locklier, who I am utterly convinced hates me, though I cannot seem to understand why. I think he was once convinced that Sam and I were together and he thought Sam broke all sorts of rules by allowing me to become involved in his investigations. I suppose Sam said as much, so we were always very discreet. Sam always told me, though, that I was able to find information he couldn't, purely because I was a civilian, and he had a reputation in the town that always preceded him..." I sighed, setting the bowl back down. "I suppose we were in the wrong, but why did officers like Locklier become as angry as they did? Wasn't it better if people's lives were saved? Or if justice was found?"

"You have no argument from me," Irene said. "Though I suppose I can see why that might threaten others, especially those in the police station." She gave me a rather pointed look over her shoulder. "If you didn't speak to Sergeant Newton, then who did you speak with?"

"You won't believe this, but Officer Chamberlin followed me out of the station, and took me to a park down Spruce Street so we could speak."

"Did he?" Irene asked. "How very interesting."

"That's what I thought," I said. "And he told me some interesting information. It seems they received the autopsy report for Sam, and what they found was quite troubling."

Irene slowly turned with the tray laden with glazed blueberry scones in her hands, her eyes widening. "Troubling? How so?"

"It seems that Sam was killed by multiple impacts made by a...a piece of glass," I said, bile rising in the back of my throat.

Irene froze as she was sliding the tray onto a rack near the door. "Glass?" she asked. "But...why? How?"

"That's what they can't understand," I said. "Chamberlin seems to think that whoever it was that killed Sam was doing their best to cover the deed up, essentially eliminating the possibility of being discovered."

"They believe someone planned this..." Irene said, coming back to the counter and taking the stool beside my own. "Someone knew what they were doing when they killed him."

"That's what Chamberlin suspects," I said. "He overheard the chief and Sergeant Newton discussing the autopsy, and heard they were worried it could very well be someone in the police station."

"One of the officers..." Irene said. "What a terrible thought."

"I know..." I said. "Chamberlin wonders if someone might have been vying for Sam's job. And after seeing the way that Locklier treated me today, I certainly wouldn't rule out him doing something awful like that."

Irene shook her head. "How could they possibly discern who is responsible?"

"Well, there was one other fear," I said. "Chamberlin also wondered whether or not it could have been someone in the military."

Irene's brow creased at that. "I don't understand," she said. "Why would someone in the military be after Sam?"

I opened my mouth, and quickly snapped it shut.

The whole reason I'd been afraid of the possibility that it was someone in the army was because it might mean the killer believed Sam knew about my involvement with everything that had happened with Roger, and Sidney, and all the rest of it.

If they somehow suspected that Sam had known what I knew, and then they killed him for it...how could I be sure the same thing wouldn't happen to Irene and her family?

I had to tread lightly, and hope that she wouldn't ask too many questions.

"Well...Chamberlin wasn't sure, but it made me wonder if somehow people believed Sam had more to do with Sidney's death than not," I said. "Given the fact Sidney was a German spy and all."

"That whole ordeal still makes so little sense to me..." Irene said. "Why in the world did he take shelter in our little village? And if he was trying to flee the war, trying to start over, then why did his superiors decide to kill him? Did he have secrets they didn't want known? Not that I am condoning his actions, of course. As a spy, he was lying to us for as long as we knew him..."

It killed me that Irene didn't know the truth. She had no idea that I'd been in Sidney's home the night he'd died, and that he'd attacked me because he thought I somehow had secrets about Roger's time as a spy...

"I..." I said.

"What's the matter?" Irene asked. "Why are you so pale all of a sudden?"

My heart began to race, and I wondered whether or not I should just continue to keep my mouth shut. I'd promised I would, didn't I?

But I could trust Irene. I know I could. And most of what I would tell her had already passed, already occurred. Would it really matter if she knew why Sidney had died?

And what if they came after Irene, the same way they'd come after Sam, if that was truly what had happened?

I chewed the inside of my lip, staring down at the counter.

"You can tell me, you know..." Irene said. "I hate seeing you so troubled."

Irene knew about Roger, of course. Not that he was still alive, but that he'd served in the military and had been high up in the ranks. In truth, even Sam hadn't known much more.

Was Roger the connecting link in all this? Was knowledge of him the reason why Sam had been killed?

And what if it wasn't the Germans that had killed him, but our own people?

Suddenly, a terrible chill passed over my body. It paralyzed me all the way to my core...and for a moment, I wasn't sure I could breathe.

"Helen?" Irene asked, concern creasing her brows. "What's the matter? Are you all right?"

My heart began to pound in my head, and fear surged through my veins.

If Roger was the one who tied this whole thing together...then how could I be sure –

How could I be sure that Roger was not the one behind this in the first place?

Behind Sam's death, behind Sidney's ultimate demise...

What if he was the one doing all this behind the scenes, completely undetected by me?

"Helen, please, what's going on? You're starting to frighten me," Irene said, her voice quiet.

I stared up at her face. "Roger..." I muttered.

Irene's brow furrowed even further. "Roger? Sweetheart, are you feeling all right? Do I need to fetch the doctor?"

"N – no," I said, the room beginning to spin. I shut my eyes, trying my best to keep present in the moment lest I lose consciousness from shock. "I'm fine, it's just – "

"You're not making any sense," Irene said. "Roger is gone, my dear. I know that all of these deaths must be terribly hard for you, but – "

I grabbed her arm, squeezing it tightly. "No, Irene. I mean Roger might be – " I said.

Irene's face fell, and her eyes widened. "Does...does all this have something to do with Roger?" she asked.

My heart skipped and I turned to look at her. It wasn't safe for her to know. If she knew, and if Roger really was the one killing all these people, and if he realized that she guessed anything –

She leaned away from me, her chest rising and falling rapidly. "I knew that something strange was going on," she said in a low voice, almost as if speaking to herself. "All this time, I knew it had something to do with Roger, but I assumed it was about his time in the army. I thought maybe you had learned something from his friend in London, or perhaps something was told to you that you couldn't repeat in the interests of the country's security – "

"That's all true," I said. "There are things that I cannot share, that I cannot say – "

"But this has something to do with Sam, too, doesn't it?" she asked. "And you've been acting very strangely when it comes to any sort of discussion about – "

"Irene, please," I said. "It isn't safe for you to know."

That thought sent a panicked shiver through me. If Roger had somehow been involved in Sam's death...but no, that was too absurd, too out of character for Roger – wasn't it?

"Why did you mention Roger, then?" Irene asked. "He couldn't have had anything to do with it. He never met Sam. You didn't meet him yourself until after Roger's death. He's been gone now for – "

Her voice trailed off, and a distant look passed over her face.

"Unless..." she said. "Unless Roger really *isn't* gone – "

"Irene, no!" I said, my voice raising more than I'd expected. "Please, do not entertain these thoughts – "

"Am I correct?" Irene asked, her eyes growing all the wider. "Is he alive, Helen?"

"I – " I said. How could I lie to her? Even in order to protect Roger?

I could lie if it meant protecting Irene and Nathanial and Michael. I had to. I had no choice.

If Roger would have gone so far as to kill Sam in order to protect himself, then how could I expect him to do any less with Irene? If she knew the truth, wouldn't she be as much of a danger as Sam was?

In reality, Irene had guessed correctly, which meant that she knew more than Sam actually had. She knew things that I wasn't even supposed to know. A government secret. A murder covered up so well that Sidney, who had attempted to kill Roger, hadn't even suspected the truth.

And now, Irene simply guessed it while we sat together in the kitchen of the teahouse because *I couldn't keep my mouth shut.*

"Helen, is this what you haven't been telling me? Is Roger actually alive?" she breathed.

I had to stop her. I had to stop this conversation before it blew out of proportion.

"I...I'm not positive," I said, and I knew that was the closest thing to the truth I could give her. In reality, I hadn't ever seen Roger with my own eyes. The only hints I had were the moments I saw his silhouette as well as the minor exchanges we'd made over the last few weeks. Even still, he'd been silent since Sam's death...

"How can you not be certain?" Irene asked. "Are you saying there is a chance of – "

"I don't know!" I snapped, and then hung my head, sighing. "I don't know," I said more gently. "There is a great deal I don't understand, but Irene, please, for my sake, please do not mention anything that we spoke about in here to anyone. Not even to Nathanial. If you do, I'm afraid it might put your family in danger."

"In danger?" Irene asked. "Why?"

"We are discussing things that we should not be," I said. "Government secrets. I just…"

I wanted to tell her. I wanted her to know that I trusted her, because I did, more than anyone else. But I needed to learn the full truth first. Needed to make sure she would be safe.

"I'm sorry," I said. "Can you promise me that?"

Irene studied my face for a long, hard moment. I could see her trust in me starting to slip, but I hoped it would hold up long enough for me to be able to figure everything out.

"I promise you I won't say anything," she said. "Not even to my own husband."

"Good," I said. "If someone caught wind of what we were talking about – "

"I could end up like Sam," Irene said.

I met her gaze, and for a moment, we exchanged understanding looks.

Yes, I thought. *You could end up just like Sam.*

12

I fled for home soon after. There had to be a way for me to contact Roger, to ask him about what was happening. I had no idea how to go about it, never having any experience writing coded messages or using different colored cloth or ink for different meanings.

I spent nearly an hour pacing back and forth in my own kitchen at home, wondering about my best course of action.

Another thought struck me as I turned for the several hundredth time on the carpet, creating grooves in the braided cloth.

What if it wasn't so much to keep his secret as it was out of jealousy?

I'd considered it when I realized that Sidney was also gone now, though he had died at my hands, not Roger's. How could I be sure that Roger hadn't orchestrated it somehow, though?

If he had, then Roger was not at all the man I thought he was...sending me into such a dangerous situation, where I had to fight my way free, killing Sidney in the process out of self defense...

How was that a demonstration of love?

It wasn't love. It was obsession. It was a territorial fight.

If Sam died because Roger had killed him out of jealousy...then Roger was not the sort of person I wanted in my life.

I couldn't be sure which thought was more troubling; that Roger might have killed Sam in order to protect his own secrets? Or out of petty jealousy?

*This is all entirely under the assumption that Roger was the one that killed Sam in the first place...*I thought, doing my best to keep myself calm. *In reality, I don't know that. I am simply troubled by the thought, and its causing me to miss out on other possible suspects.*

I chewed on the inside of my lip, forcing myself to push thoughts of Roger out of my mind. It was impossible, though, as those horrible ideas continued to appear unbidden in my streams of thought.

Finally, I realized that perhaps the best thing for me to do was to go again and investigate the place where Sam had been found. In the daylight. It was possible I'd missed something in the darkness of night, and now knowing that Sam had been killed with a piece of glass...

I stopped short, nearly tripping over a wrinkle in the rug beneath my feet.

*A piece of glass...*I thought. *Wasn't there a broken window in the upper story of the Mayfield's home?*

My heart began to race. Was it at all possible that a piece from that broken window had been used to kill Sam?

Maybe it was still there. Maybe the police hadn't found the other part of the shard, the part that hadn't broken off into Sam when he'd been stabbed.

I still didn't like the thought of Sam being so brutally killed...I tried not to imagine how lonely he must have been as he died.

As I located my coat, hanging down from the hook in my shop downstairs, I wondered what his last thoughts might have been.

Was he afraid? I wondered as I pulled one of the sleeves on. *I certainly would have been.*

I hoped he hadn't been in too much pain, or that he hadn't lain there for hours before he died, nothing but the chill of the night to keep his company.

I knew it was quite certain he had suffered to some degree. How could someone be pierced so many times and not suffer? It had been enough to kill him, after all...

*How could someone do this...*I thought, just as I had so many times before over the last few weeks.

As I stepped out onto High Street, I furrowed my brow.

Roger, I hope more than anything that it wasn't you, I thought, my hands sliding into the pockets of my jacket. *I hope it wasn't you, and I honestly don't know what I would do if it was.*

Pushing those thoughts away once more, I set my eyes on Mr. Hodgins' butcher shop, and the house I knew had been empty for the last few weeks while the Mayfields had been gone visiting their son.

The alleyway was just as I remembered it. Even in the daylight, it was clear there was very little back there. Nothing more than some rubbish bins, old and broken wooden boxes, and the well-traveled path winding behind the houses and shops.

Setting my hands on my hips, I looked around near the Mayfield's home.

The window was still broken, though it looked as though it hadn't been damaged by too much more since I'd seen it last. Rain and wind perhaps, and I hoped nothing inside had been ruined any more than it might have been by the person who had broken in.

I wandered over underneath the window, peering at the overgrown grass that encircled the house.

Tiny shards glinted in the moody, dull grey light of the afternoon.

Using the tip of my shoe, I pushed them around, looking for any evidence of blood or cloth, yet I found nothing.

Was it possible that Sam's murder and the person who had broken into the house had nothing to do with each other?

No...that seemed like far too much of a coincidence, and I wasn't one to believe in coincidences.

I liked the theory of the person breaking into the house being the same one who killed Sam, as it likely eliminated the possibility of Roger being the murderer. What purpose would Roger have breaking into someone's home? I could think of nothing, though it certainly made me wonder where he'd been sleeping over the last few months...

I dragged a partially empty rubbish bin beneath the window, and crawled up on top, the metal lid groaning underneath my weight.

I steadied myself by laying my hands against the

honey-colored wall of the house, and stared upward until I felt my legs stop trembling.

The window was still mostly out of reach, but if I were to climb up onto the overhang above the window on the lower floor...

This is crazy, I told myself as I laid my hands on top of the tile overhang, hoisting myself into the air, and pulling my body up onto it. *If I get caught, I am going to be in all sorts of trouble.*

I tried not to think about that as I looked up at the broken window, and realized I could reach it now.

Laying my hands on the windowsill, I hissed through my teeth as I yanked my fingers back down toward myself. Tiny, sharp stings shot through my hands, like the sting of a dozen bees.

When I overturned my hands, I saw little shards of glass had pierced through my tender skin.

A cold wave of nausea passed through me. Why hadn't I considered there might be more broken glass up there?

Carefully, I plucked each piece of glass from my fingers, realizing it looked more frightening than it actually was; the skin hadn't been broken more than three times.

Pulling my jacket off, I wrapped it around my hands before attempting to lift myself up once again.

It was easier this time, as I could rest my feet on the top of the overhang beneath me, and could see inside just enough to make out a beautifully decorated bedroom in the room beyond.

The room itself wasn't all that big, but everything was

dark apart from what little light the windows would allow inside.

A tall dresser with a mirror stood against the northern wall, and a pretty carved desk waited patiently for someone to occupy it's chair beside the door that must have led out into the rest of the house. The drawers had all been pulled out, and papers settled over the floor and the sides of the desk.

The nightstands, too, on either side of the bed, seemed to have had their drawers upended, their contents scattered about on the floor. Combs, spools of thread, books, and small bottles of perfume lay jumbled together, clearly not the object of the thief's intentions.

None of those held my attention for long, because I noticed the shattered pieces of glass strewn about on the floor beneath the window, and it was clear from the sheer amount of it that the window had been broken inward, not outward.

Whoever had broken in had climbed up here, likely in the same way I had.

The jagged pieces of glass still in the window frame looked menacing, and as I stared at them, along with the ones lying on the floor, it was easy to see how they could have been used alternatively as a weapon.

The two crimes have to be connected, I thought as I glanced back down at the ground behind me. *Whoever broke in here had to be the one to kill Sam.*

I was beginning to doubt my own discernment in all this. There were too many possibilities, especially given my new revelation that it could have been Roger that killed Sam.

This seemed more plausible, though, didn't it?

Someone had been sneaking into the house, and Sam had somehow caught them in the act. In fear or anger, the burglar had attacked Sam, perhaps not intending to kill but only wound, and then fled...

That seemed the most likely, didn't it?

Then why were the police worried it could have been an inside job? Or perhaps even someone military?

Was it possible it was much simpler than we had all thought? Could it have been nothing more than that Sam was at the wrong place at the wrong time?

As I gingerly crawled down off the overhang and back onto the rubbish bin lid, I wondered if Sergeant Newton had even come here to check the house. Likely not, or the glass would have been cleaned up by now.

I wasn't quite sure what to think about all this. I did know that it was beginning to hurt my head, though, and I wasn't sure where to go from here.

This wasn't even enough evidence. I had no names, no faces, no witnesses...how could I possibly locate someone who had been here weeks ago, and had managed to slip away without detection?

I stared up at the window, my heart sinking.

The sound of a heavy door sliding closed further along the alleyway caught my attention, causing me to turn around.

In the next building over, the butcher's shop, I saw a sliver of light peeking through the gap between the metal door and the frame just as it was closing.

My heart began to beat quickly once more.

Had someone been watching me?

I'd been almost positive that I'd been alone in this alleyway, not having seen hide nor hair of anyone since climbing up on that rubbish bin. With the buildings as close together as they were, I certainly wouldn't have missed it.

You're being paranoid, I told myself. *It could have very well been Mr. Hodgins simply taking out the garbage. Given how hard the man works, he likely wouldn't have seen me, even if he had been looking.*

Nevertheless, I couldn't shake the prickling along my spine as I made my way from the alleyway. What if someone *had* been watching me?

What if it had been Roger?

I hurried home, my head spinning as I tried to keep my thoughts straight.

There certainly seemed to be more to this mystery than I had ever thought possible. Whoever had killed Sam was doing a bang up job at keeping their identity hidden. I had no earthly idea who it could have been, nor did the police seem to know.

Would this go down as yet another unsolved murder? While Sam had been alive, there had been no such thing. In his absence, now, though...were we more likely to fail?

*I'm sorry, Sam...*I thought. *I'm so very sorry.*

13

I had a difficult time sleeping that night. Over and over in my mind, I kept playing the image of Sam lying dead in that alleyway, broken shards of glass protruding from his bloodied body.

In the morning, as I sat at the foot of my bed staring out at the rooftops across the street, I realized that I was letting Sam down. He had come to put his trust in me before he'd died, purely through my ability to solve problems that were just out of his reach. We'd come to make a good team, and for now, I felt as if I was not upholding his trust in me.

"What would you say to me if you were here, Sam?" I asked, staring down at the fraying edge of the blanket I had wrapped around my shoulders.

That was an interesting question, wasn't it? What would he say?

I tugged at the end of one of the strings hanging from my blanket.

"Well, you probably would tell me that I needed to

stop and think about everything I've learned so far," I said. "And you would remind me that it would be better if I just stayed out of this in the first place. Surely, though, you would know that I would tell you I had no intention of ducking out now, especially when I've already invested so much time in this..."

I sighed.

"You'd probably tell me to pay attention to what everyone had said, but also to not trust anyone. You would tell me it is most likely that someone, somewhere, is lying to me, and that I need to do what I can in order to find this person."

I blinked, my eyelids heavy.

But I couldn't stay here. I needed to get up and do what I could for the day.

"There has to be something I'm overlooking," I said on the telephone to Irene, who I'd called to share some of my woes for the day.

She seemed annoyed at first, especially about everything I'd said, or not said, about Roger the day before, but quickly forgave me when I told her how torn up I was about all this. I apologized at least seven more times as well, just for good measure. "You know, sometimes the best way to look at a problem is to set it aside for some time and come back to it later with fresh eyes," she said. "You've been agonizing over this for weeks now, Helen. It's no wonder you're tired out and upset. Have you thought about taking any time away? Even just for an afternoon?"

It was not something I had considered, not at all.

"Perhaps you are right..." I said. "But where would I go? It isn't as if I would want to take the train all the way into Plymouth. How would I explain to my parents all that's happened recently? What would that do but worry them?"

"What about taking a trip just outside of town?" Irene asked. "There are some lovely castles and ruins in this part of the country. Maybe you would enjoy going out into the countryside. Have some fresh air, clear your mind."

"Irene, you are a wonderful friend," I said. "You are always thinking of me and wanting to take care of me. Something like that never crossed my mind, but to be frank, it sounds wonderful."

"Then perhaps it is precisely what you should do," Irene said. "Your shop will still be here, as will the rest of us here in town. You need to take care of yourself through all of this, all right? We don't want you to completely lose your sense of self."

"I really don't know how to apologize enough for how I acted yesterday..." I said.

"It's quite all right, dear," Irene said, though there was a definite note of curtness in her voice. "I do hope that one day you will find that you can indeed trust me."

"I do trust you, Irene," I said. "And I care about you. That's why I'm choosing to keep most of this a secret right now. It really is for your own safety."

"I know," Irene said. "And I do trust you. I understand you wouldn't have said what you said without reason. I realize it's entirely possible that everything to do with... well, your late husband, really, is above what I should know. I don't have to know everything, and that's all right. It's something I realized last night. I didn't have to be so hard on you. I should have been much more supportive."

"Thank you, Irene," I said. "I appreciate it."

Irene gave me directions to one of the nearest castles, and I found myself invigorated by the idea of spending a day away from Brookminster.

I realized that part of my anxiety about this whole ordeal was that I just wanted to control the situation. That wasn't a complete surprise, but to realize that in me was a big development in terms of my character.

Getting a chance to take a step back seemed to be the best choice for me, and Irene was right. It might be just the thing I needed in order to clear my head.

THE CASTLE WASN'T ALL that far outside of town. George, Irene's brother, was ready and willing to take me, as well as talk to me all about his newest pursuit, which happened to be funneling items that were needed for the war, like papers and ink and other necessities, from town to the train station.

When we reached our destination and he asked if I wanted him to pick me up again, I said that I certainly did, but wanted a few hours to explore the castle. Seemingly all too happy to hear it, he agreed to come just before sundown, when I would then head back home, hopefully after some much needed time of rejuvenation.

A kind woman at the gate house allowed me entrance, and after paying a few pence for admission, I wandered in to the castle's courtyard.

It had once belonged to a Lord, far back in the early seventeenth century. The signs scattered about the place told tales of daring sword fights, lavish feasts, and elaborate balls that were once held within the castle's walls.

There was a great deal that was still intact, but much of the northern side of the castle was nothing more than a crumbling ruin. Careful to avoid any gaps in stairwells, I headed toward the watchtower at the northeastern side of the castle.

It was much quieter out here. There hadn't been any other guests through that day. The woman at the front gate had said as much. "Hardly any visitors out this far, given the state of the war," she said. "It's not a great surprise, though. We are hoping everything will go back to normal once the war is over."

The idea of the war being over seemed so far out of reach that it was difficult to imagine. How was it possible that it had been going as long as it had? Every day, so many were giving up their lives. Families were forever changed, and for what? I could see no good in any of it.

The castle was beautiful, and it was a shame that no one was there to enjoy it.

Although...I'm not entirely upset that I am able to explore this place to my heart's content, all on my own. It almost makes me feel like a princess...

The watch tower had spectacular views of the surrounding rolling hills and the valley. The trees were all changing in a beautiful array of colors, like the sunset had shed its colors across the landscape in order to preserve its own glory.

In the distance, Brookminster had begun to come to life as the sun headed toward the horizon in the west. Warm lights glittered from the windows, like tiny pinpricks, glowing in invitation. The houses and shops looked like the picture perfect scene, and so comfortable that I wondered why I had wanted to run away from there in the first place.

Everything was so peaceful up here, in the cool evening air, with the gentle breeze brushing against my face. I could have stood up here for the rest of my life, just taking in the view.

Irene was right. This was precisely what I needed.

Why was I so utterly consumed with dread when I was back in Brookminster? Out here, in the open air, everything felt so much smaller. Even my fear about Sam's case seemed to have shrunken in size in my heart.

I took in deep gulps of the air, relishing the freedom that seeped into my bones. When was the last time I'd been alone like this? And in more than just my own home? When had I taken a step back from everything and just allowed myself to be?

I couldn't recall, and realized that I needed to do it more often.

A footstep scuffed against the stone floor behind me.

A chill ran down my spine, and then the wind went out of my sails. *Oh well. It was nice to be alone while I had the chance.*

I moved closer to the crumbled wall, careful to stay behind the designated lines, and continued to stare out over the valley. The moment of peace was gone, though, having been snatched away by whoever had decided to come up to the tower instead of exploring the rest of the castle, of which there was much.

The footsteps behind me moved closer, and I turned to look over my shoulder.

A young man stood there, and it only took me a moment to realize I recognized him.

"Oh," I said. "Hello there. Arthur, wasn't it? Victoria's son?" I asked.

He was taller than I remembered, with a layer of fuzz around his jawline that hadn't been there when I'd met him a few weeks before.

"Yeah," he said, his hands deep in the pockets of his jacket.

"Out here to enjoy the view as well, hmm?" I asked, turning to look out over the valley.

"No," he said. "I'm here to see you."

The edge in his words made the small hairs on the back of my neck stand straight up. "See...me?" I asked. "Why would you want to do that?"

He took a step toward me, and a gust of wind blew across the top of the watchtower.

He didn't answer, but his gaze was hard, his clear, blue eyes fixed on me.

I took another step back, and beneath my heel, some of the stones shifted, causing my stomach to summersault.

"I saw you out behind the butcher shop yesterday," Arthur said, his tone flat, yet the stiffness in his shoulders told me he must have been attempting to keep his anger in check. "Why do you keep hanging out around there?"

My heart started to beat hard, slamming against my ribs.

I didn't imagine the door closing at the butcher's, then...

"You heard that Sam Graves was killed back there, right?" I asked, doing my best not to jump to conclusions. "He...was a dear friend of mine. I said I would do all I could to help him, and I feel that helping find the person who killed him is my last effort to do just that."

He made a sound like a grunt, kicking out with his foot against a loose stone, sending it flying across the top of the watchtower. It clattered past me and tumbled down into the open air, only to fall three stories down to the ground below.

"I'm sorry, but why is this such a troubling thing to you?" I asked. "Why do you seem so put off by it? It has utterly no effect on you."

Arthur stared blankly at me, a tightness around his eyes that made me stop and wonder what was going through his mind.

"It...it shouldn't have any effect on me," he said. "You're right. I...it never should have...I didn't mean for..."

My heart was hammering so hard against my ribs that I was certain he'd be able to hear it.

No...I thought. *It can't be. He's not trying to admit that he* –

"He never should have walked into the alleyway that night..." Arthur said, his gaze fixed on the rocky stone floor between us. "If he'd just stayed away, then this never would have – "

Heart sinking, I stared across the watchtower. "You... you killed Sam..."

Arthur's clear eyes flickered up to meet mine, a perplexed look on his face. "He shouldn't have interfered..."

"What happened?" I asked, taking a step toward him. "How did you – "

"I was climbing out of the window of the Mayfield's house..." Arthur said in a rather mystified voice. "They were gone, had left that afternoon. I watched them pile their luggage into the cab and drive off. I thought it was the perfect chance for me to sneak in and see what sort of valuables they could do without."

My brow furrowed at his flippant remark. "What sort of valuables they...you knew perfectly well what you were doing, then. And certainly have no remorse for it."

"Why would I?" he asked. "Done that dozens of times before. People like the Mayfields have so much wealth, they won't miss a few trinkets. People like me, though... we could certainly use the extra help."

"But you don't steal to get that sort of help," I said. "You work hard for it, just like everyone else – "

"Work hard?" he asked. "What am I supposed to do when no one would hire me because of my reputation? It was never my fault that the other boys in town thought they were better than me and saw nothing wrong with pushing me around and making fun of me. For my clothes, my father's job..."

His brow knit together, and a dark look passed over his face.

"I told myself, even back then, that I would prove them wrong. I would find a way to be better than them. I already was better than them, but they just couldn't see it. They didn't understand..."

He looked out over toward Brookminster in the fading light of the day.

"No one ever understood me. That's why they put me in boarding school, and everyone there hated me, too. So I wanted to learn how to get back at them, to cause them the sort of pain they'd caused me. I learned how to steal, and I got better at it every year. Students started losing pocket change, but slowly, bigger things went missing, and my closets and boxes beneath my bed were filling with the spoils of my endeavors. I realized it was something I was good at, and pretty soon, it was all I knew how to do."

I had no way to counteract what the boy was saying. He was too lost in his own pain to ever hear my correction, and would never listen if I told him that what he was doing was so utterly wrong.

"When I came home from school, my mother insisted I join the army. When I refused, knowing she couldn't force me, then she made me get a job. Mr. Hodgins wasn't easy to please, but he also seemed to understand me in a way no one else did...so I started working for him."

My heart skipped. I wasn't sure I wanted to hear the rest of the story, having a sneaking suspicion that I already knew how it would unfold.

"I started to wonder if I might actually be able to make a decent living working at a real job," Arthur said, defeat clear on his face. "I actually *like* working for Mr. Hodgins. He's taught me a lot. He trusts me with a great deal, and I don't want to let him down."

I pursed my lips, biting back the words that wanted to come. He'd found someone who was willing to try and whip him into shape...but was it too late?

"Then I heard the Mayfield's were going out of town," he said. "The temptation came back, and it was too strong to resist. I promised myself I was only going to take a look, make it my last time, but I didn't expect him to catch me like he did..."

"Sam..." I said. "You're talking about Sam."

The last of the sun fell down below the horizon,

bathing the southern part of the tower in shadows from the fallen, broken rock wall. Arthur stood just beyond the pool of darkness, his pale face turned upward toward me. "Yes," he said. "I'm talking about the Inspector. He caught me as I was leaving the Mayfield's, and tried to stop me. I realized that if I was caught, I'd end up in prison, and I'd done so much to avoid being taken to prison. I hadn't even taken anything. I tried to explain this to the Inspector, but he would not listen. He just tried to grab me and drag me down to the police station."

He lifted a trembling hand to his face, which he rubbed nervously.

"I...I'm still not sure how it happened. One moment he was standing there, yelling at me. Then he whirled away, dragging me along behind him. Next thing I knew, a shard of glass from the window was in my hand, slicing into my fingers as I jabbed it into him in order to make him release me. I...I couldn't stop. I just kept striking him, over and over, until his screaming stopped..."

His hand fell to his side, and for a moment, he himself looked like nothing more than a corpse standing there.

"...But the screaming never stopped," he said. "It's always in my head, ringing over and over again. No matter what I do, I can't silence it – "

He pressed his palms flat against either side of his head as if he meant to pop it like a grape, his face long, his eyes growing wild.

"It was over so fast, and before I even had a chance to regret it, he was gone."

My head pounded, and my mouth had gone dry.

It was his fault Sam was gone. And yet, I couldn't find

it in me to be as angry as I expected to be. He was just a child, after all. Barely out of his youth...and now with this awful deed hanging over him –

A flash of silver caught my attention, down near Arthur's hip.

A thin knife had been pulled from his pocket. Something sharp enough to cut through bone and sinew.

"I know your screams will haunt me, too..." he said, taking a step toward me. "But I can't have you running back to the police with everything I've just told you. What would I do then? How would I go on?"

The knife glinted as he lifted it higher, and for a moment, it was as if I could feel its sting across my flesh.

A shadow appeared behind Arthur, tall and hulking, and before I could open my mouth to warn him, hands stretched out of the darkness and wrapped around Arthur's throat.

14

I let out a cry as the hands wrapped around Arthur yanked him backward into the shadows.

Fear washed over me as the sound of scuffling reached me, of two men grunting and wrestling.

What if it's a robber? Or another criminal? Here I am, entirely defenseless –

I had no choice. I had to make a run for it.

I charged toward the southern side of the tower, where the only staircase leading up to the roof was located. I had to get away before either of them could reach me. I had the confession I needed, all I had to do was make it back to the station and tell Sergeant Newton –

I heard a sickening cry from behind me, and chanced a look over my shoulder. The larger man had grabbed Arthur by the back of his shirt, lifting him as easily as if he were a doll, and thrown him out of the shadows. I watched in horror as the screaming young man flew over the roof's edge and plunged over the side of the tower.

As Arthur fell out of my sight, a gasp stole all the breath from my lungs.

Silence followed, a long, deafening silence.

How many heartbeats did he have left? One? Perhaps two?

Then I heard the *thud* as he struck the bottom, landing among the broken stones of the crumbling tower.

I sank down to my knees, terror welling up inside of me like a vice around my heart.

He...he was just here. He was never supposed to die. I didn't want him to die!

My eyes fell upon the man who had killed him...and my fear warped into some sort of twisted fascination.

For a brief, utterly insane moment, I thought it might be Sam, given his build and height, and his dark hair. But it only took me a fraction of a heartbeat to realize that no, it wasn't Sam, but he was certainly a man that I recognized.

I got to my feet, my knees shaky as I gawked at the back of his head.

A moment later, he turned around, and my knees threatened to give way beneath me once again.

It had been seven months since I'd seen his face, and yet, it came back to me as clearly as if I'd seen him yesterday. That scar over his right eye was still there, partially obscured by his full, dark brows. His nose, slightly bent from being broken more than once, and his high cheekbones, all were exactly as I remembered.

But it was his gaze, which latched onto me like a magnet, that drew the tears to my eyes.

"Roger..." I breathed, and without hesitating, ran forward toward him, my arms outstretched.

Every frantic heartbeat that passed as I hurried toward him sent fear through me. What if this wasn't real? What if I was hallucinating it all, imagining him standing there before me?

It wasn't a dream, though.

I threw myself into his arms, which he wrapped around me without hesitation.

And then I cried. I cried so hard and for so long that I lost the ability to stand. I clung to him, dug my fingernails into his back, fearing that if I blinked, if I released my iron grip on him for even a moment, that he'd vanish and I would never see him again.

"There, there, my love..." he whispered, running his calloused fingers through my chestnut hair, just like he always used to when I was upset. "It's all right, now. I'm here. You don't have to cry."

But I couldn't stop, not for some time. Seven months of grief and agony poured out of me until there was no strength left within my soul.

"There, now..." he said.

I pulled away from him, keeping my arms securely locked behind his neck, and stared up into his face. "It really is you..." I breathed. "I was...I was so certain it was you, but I never wanted to let myself hope, not too much, fearing that I would have to suffer losing you again – "

He pressed his lips to mine, and it was as if an explosion went off inside my mind. Every one of my nerves sang in triumph, and the blood rushed in my ears, making me dizzy.

"Helen...I am so sorry..." he said a moment later, pressing his forehead to mine, keeping me as close as possible. "These seven months have been torture for me.

I was absolutely furious with my superiors for making me lie to you like they did. I knew it would break you, and it broke me to have to watch you suffer through the funeral and the phone call...I hated that they wouldn't let me tell you the truth."

"But why wouldn't they?" I asked. "How can you reveal yourself to me now?"

"I shouldn't," he said. "But this may be the only place where no one will see or hear us. When I saw you getting into that cab, I overheard you mention the castle to Irene's brother – yes, I'm aware of the names of everyone you know – and I knew it might be my only chance to speak with you. And aren't I glad I came, because if I hadn't who knows what that boy might have done to you..."

A chill ran down my spine. "He killed Sam."

"I know," Roger said.

I looked up into Roger's face, the tears returning. "Oh, Roger, can you ever forgive me? There was a short time where I thought it might have been you, attempting to keep your secret safe, or perhaps out of – out of – "

"Out of what?" he asked.

"Jealousy," I said.

He kissed my forehead, and then the tip of my nose. "My darling, if you had found another man to love when you were convinced I was dead, how could I have blamed you for it? It would have killed me, but my superiors warned me that it might happen, but that I was still not to interfere... But I had noticed the way Sam Graves was looking at you when you didn't know he was looking, and knew I had to do what I could to get you to notice me."

"That's why you let me catch you that day in the alley?" I asked. "Because of jealousy?"

"I suppose it was," Roger said sheepishly.

Darkness had fallen properly over the tower, and the only lights up where we were came from further inside the castle and from the few lights in the courtyard on the other side of the property.

Roger hugged me against himself once again. "Helen I am terribly sorry, but I cannot linger here long. I am meant to travel to London tonight to give my reports – "

"Reports on what?" I asked.

"I've been tracking any associates of Sidney Mason's," Roger said. "I'm sorry you had to go through all of that. I had hoped to find a way to eliminate him, but you certainly have become quite a detective, haven't you? You snuck into his house one evening when I wasn't around and hadn't seen you."

"Yes..." I said, relief washing over me at finally being able to tell someone. "I killed him. In self-defense."

"Oh, Helen..." Roger said. "You never should have had to endure anything like that."

"It's all right," I said. "I'm fine. Perhaps shaken up about it all still, but he wasn't who I thought he was."

"No," Roger said. "And I'm sorry that a great deal of what's happened to you the last year has been that way. Not as it seemed."

I embraced him once again, knowing that our time now was short.

"I must go, Helen," Roger said in a low murmur. "And I know that you have news to report to others, as well. You must not tell anyone about me, though. It will be best if they believe this young man slipped – "

"That is precisely what I was thinking as well," I said. "Don't worry. I've protected your secret thus far, and I won't falter now."

He kissed me once again. "I love you dearly, you know that, yes?"

I closed my eyes for a moment, savoring the words as they rang in my mind. "And I love you..." I breathed in reply. I still couldn't believe he was here.

He squeezed my hand tightly, and I knew that it was time to go.

"Roger, what are we to do now?" I asked. "I can't go back to a life without you. Why must I keep pretending?"

He looked down at me, and that sweet, small smile appeared on his face that I loved so dearly. "Do not fear, my love. Roger Lightholder must remain dead for the time being. With my current assignments, it is necessary for me to stay undercover. It will allow me to work better this way."

I had feared he might say that.

"But know that this is only temporary. It is just until after the war, after which we can be together."

My eyes widened. "Truly? After the war is over?"

He nodded. "When the war is over, I have been given permission to step back into my life. At that time, it won't matter. I will of course have to be under some sort of supervision, but that is only in case some of the enemy who might not have been captured or killed still come after me. I will likely have to take on a different name, but for our families and friends, they will know that I'm alive."

"Take a different name..." I said.

Roger grinned at me. "I suppose that means I will

have to just happen into your life one day and sweep you off your feet as I did once before. To the rest of the world, you will have happily moved on from your late husband's passing. To us, it will be just picking up where we left off."

The idea certainly intrigued me.

"But we must go now, Helen," Roger said. "You must tell the police about the butcher's assistant's attack on you, and his confession to killing Sam Graves. At least there will be one less mystery to solve in this crazy world."

"You're right," I said. My thoughts drifted to the body now lying at the bottom of the tower. "His family...what a terrible night they are about to have."

"Do not take on the burdens of others as your own, dear one," Roger murmured. "There is no reason why you must carry all that pain as well."

"I know." I said.

We walked hand in hand as far as we could, before Roger glanced down a long, dark passage in the castle.

"I must leave through one of the back doors," he said. "No one can know that I was here."

"Of course," I said.

He pulled me into his arms once again, kissing me deeply.

"I love you," he whispered.

"And I love you," I said, knowing I meant it more now than I ever had before in my life.

EPILOGUE

"Mrs. Lightholder, could I bother you for a moment?"

"Of course, Mrs. Georgianna, what can I help you with?"

It was the third of October, and the weather had been pleasantly cool. The countryside was preparing itself for winter, with the farmers harvesting their crops and the sheep enjoying the last bits of green grass scattered along the hillsides.

The townsfolk of Brookminster, too, were scurrying about, readying themselves for winter. Many of the ladies were doing their best to preserve the last of the autumn's harvest, from the apples to the squash, they and their husbands did what they could to ensure their families could survive through the winter.

Some were frightened the war might make the transfer of goods rather complicated in the bitter winter months. Most, though, were optimistic, as they knew how to prepare.

"I was wondering if you had any of these buttons, but perhaps in a deep blue?" Mrs. Georgianna asked me as I met her at the small, round table where I'd been keeping the newest arrival of buttons.

"Oh, how clever of you, Miss Georgianna," I said with a smile at the older woman. "I certainly do have some blue buttons. How did you know that they arrived yesterday?"

She grinned at me. "Well, I thought I overheard you saying something to Mrs. Driscoll, and that sort of blue would be so fetching with my new coat I just finished."

"A new coat, you say?" I asked as I made my way back to the storage closet. "I suppose there is no better time than now to have that prepared, hmm? I should like to see it sometime."

"Of course, I shall wear it on the next unseasonably cold day we have," she said.

I smiled as I dipped into the storage closet, pulling free some of the boxes I'd received just the day before.

I heard the bell chime above the door, and Irene's voice trickled in after it.

"Hello, Mrs. Georgianna, fancy seeing you here," Irene said.

"Oh come now, Irene, I'm here very nearly every day for one project or another," Mrs. Georgianna said. "If I wasn't quite so forgetful, I might be able to make it a few days before needing to return for something."

Irene laughed.

I reappeared with the box of blue buttons and carried them out. "Hello, Irene," I said. "How are you doing today?"

"Oh quite well, of course," she said, beaming at me. "Is it ready?"

I grinned at the glee on her pretty face. "It certainly is," I said.

I ushered her toward the back of the shop with me, noting Mrs. Georgianna's curious stares after us, even as she ran her fingers through the box of buttons.

I picked up a small, golden box on the counter beside the till, and passed it to her.

Irene's face split into a broad smile as she lifted the top, and gasped. "Oh, Helen, it's lovely...he is going to absolutely love it."

"Go on and open it," I said.

Irene reached inside and pulled out a gold pocket watch. It was handsomely made with an intricate carving of a crown of ivy on the front. She popped it open, and her eyes filled with tears.

I leaned around to see it once more.

"*To Nathanial, my wonderful husband and soon to be father to two wonderful children.*"

"Helen, it's perfect..." she said, smiling at me with tears glittering in her eyes.

"And you don't think he suspects anything?" I asked.

Irene shook her head. "Not yet, no. He keeps wondering when I am going to get over this stomach ache I've been dealing with, but it's been so long since we had Michael, I'm not sure he remembers much of what my first pregnancy was like." She gazed down at the watch once again. "Who did the engraving?"

"I tried my hand at it," I said. "Does it look all right?"

"It's wonderful," Irene said.

"And the silk in the box is from an old tie here that

never sold," I said. "Perhaps a bit garish for most men, but I think it looks lovely sitting inside that box."

"Oh, it certainly does," Irene said. She closed the lid on the box.

"The chain is brand new as well," I said. "I went through several different boxes of watches that my aunt never managed to sell and found the best one."

"I'm so pleased..." Irene said.

"As am I!" I said, smiling at her. "It's absolutely wonderful."

"Now, what do I owe you for all this?" she asked.

"Nothing," I said, taking a step back from her.

"You cannot be serious," she said, her grey eyes shadowed by her now furrowed brow. "Helen, I must give you something for all this – "

"Nonsense," I said. "It's his birthday present, isn't it? And with your big news, I imagine you are going to need all the extra money you can save."

Irene's face fell, but she threw her arms around me and gave me a tight hug.

"Thank you..." she said. "This is one of the best gifts I've ever received."

I smiled as I hugged her in return. "I am happy to do it," I said. "I wouldn't be much of a friend if I couldn't help you out from time to time."

She changed the subject, then. "How about you? Have you heard from...well, you know," she asked.

I grinned.

After telling Sergeant Newton about Arthur Barnes' confession to murdering Sam Graves, I had hurried to tell Irene what happened...and to come clean about Roger. I had asked him, after all, if I was allowed to tell her, and only her, the truth, just before we parted ways.

He hadn't been entirely thrilled with the idea, but he agreed to it nevertheless, knowing that I would need someone to confide in, lest I entirely lost sense of myself with all the secrets I was keeping. "But nothing about what I'm doing," he instructed. "That must remain secret."

It hadn't been hard to agree to, and when I admitted it to her, she'd been overjoyed with me that Roger was still, in fact, very much alive.

"His most recent note was tucked away inside a boot on my front step," I said. "And it was entirely in Italian."

"Italian?" Irene said. "Do you even read Italian?"

"Not in the slightest," I said, shrugging my shoulders. "Ever since he and I have found these secret, hidden ways of speaking with one another, I think he's been rather amused to give me something more challenging each time."

"It certainly seems that way," Irene said with a grin.

"I shall have to spend hours at the library, in hopes of finding a decent language book to translate it," I said.

Irene and I laughed together, and my heart was full. My closest friend and her husband were going to have another baby, and I was reconnecting with my husband, slowly but surely.

Life, it seemed, was still quite good, despite the ups and downs we'd experienced over the last several months.

"And what of this new side business?" Irene asked, leaning against the counter, folding her arms. "How has that been?"

I glanced over at Mrs. Georgianna, who was doing nothing to hide the fact that she was listening in on our conversation.

I smiled at Irene. "It's quite good. I have my first appointment this afternoon. Mrs. Trent, believe it or not."

"Really?" Irene asked. "I wonder what sort of stories she wants to tell..."

"What's this about a new side business?" Mrs. Georgianna asked. "What are you up to?"

I smiled. "I'm not up to anything, Mrs. Georgianna. Truthfully, it isn't so much a business as a service I hope to offer. I simply realized that everyone has a story to tell, and sometimes it is better for them to be able to have their stories heard than for them to build up and become problems for them in the future. For instance, I believe that if Arthur Barnes had been able to tell his troubles to someone, he might not have felt the need to break into the Mayfield's home, which then put him in the position of killing Inspector Graves...He told me some rather sad truths about his life, and I think a great deal of it is what led him to the choices he made. I want to give people the chance to share their struggles, to talk it over with someone, before it makes them react poorly down the road."

"How wise of you..." Mrs. Georgianna said.

"I am not certain it will work," I said. "But I do know that I would like to see Brookminster return to the quiet, cozy village that it always has been."

It would be difficult, I knew. With Sam gone, I still had the desire to help people. Seeing others grieving and losing their loved ones, I realized there had to be a better way.

Perhaps this could work as a preventative measure, I

thought, and it gave me hope. Hope that there could be an end to the darkness that seemed to have taken hold in Brookminster.

The world certainly seemed brighter, these days, even amidst the stories about the war that still streamed in through the papers. In such times it was best to find joy where one could, while we all waited together for a better future – one I felt confident would eventually come.

Travel back to the 1920s to begin another historical mystery series from Blythe Baker, starting with "A Subtle Murder: The Rose Beckingham Murder Mysteries, Book 1."

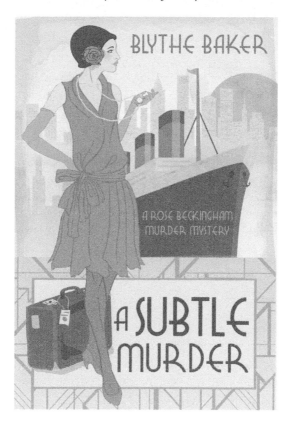

ABOUT THE AUTHOR

Blythe Baker is the lead writer behind several popular historical and paranormal mystery series. When Blythe isn't buried under clues, suspects, and motives, she's acting as chauffeur to her children and head groomer to her household of beloved pets. She enjoys walking her dog, lounging in her backyard hammock, and fiddling with graphic design. She also likes binge-watching mystery shows on TV.

To learn more about Blythe, visit her website and sign up for her newsletter at www.blythebaker.com